CRUSH 2

TEXT **KINGPUB** to **22828** to join the **King Publishing Group** mailing list!
Free book giveaways, event dates and much more!

CRUSH 2

IVY SYMONE

Chapter 1

Jazmin was frozen with emotions. She wasn't sure if she should flee to avoid what was to come or stay and get everything over with. After all, this was what she'd been wanting out of Sean, just for him to tell the truth.

Her mouth became dry as it gaped open waiting on the awkward silence between Sean and Rayven to be over. Sean stared at his wife as she looked at him with an expression of hurt and disbelief.

"What did you just say, Sean?" Rayven asked again.

With slight uneasiness, Sean replied quietly, "It was nothing."

Rayven's disappointment and devastation seemed to fade and was replaced with fury. She stepped up to him until they were inches apart. "It was nothing like I didn't hear you say anything, or it was nothing like whatever you have going on with Jazmin is nothing?"

"What are you talking about?" Sean asked with feigned confusion.

Rayven's head snapped around in Jazmin's direction. "Are you fucking my husband?"

Before Jazmin could utter a sound, Sean intervened with a nervous laugh, "C'mon bae! Don't do that. You know I would never do that."

Unable to contain her emotions, Rayven yelled angrily, "Then why are you over here! Why are you saying things to Jah about losing Jazmin to him? Why, Sean?"

Desiree looked over at Jazmin with question. Jazmin avoided her gaze; her body language confessing to guilt. With disgust and devastation, Desiree asked, "Really Jazz?"

Jazmin retorted, "Really what, Dez?"

Rayven whipped her head back in Jazmin's direction. "So you did?"

There was silence.

With her voice cracking, Rayven asked, "So you've been fucking my husband?"

Jazmin glanced in Jah's direction. He leaned up against the hallway wall with his arms folded over his chest. "What'chu looking over here for? This y'all shit."

Sean looked at Jah as if he could kill him. "Really, Jah?"

"Really Jah my ass," Jah snapped. "You had no business bringing yo' stupid ass over here with that bullshit. She tried to tell you yo' wife was upstairs, dumb ass nigga."

Rayven let out a deranged laugh and palmed her forehead with a loud smack. "Oh my God! So you've been fucking Jazmin. Isn't this great! Did you know, Dez?"

"No!" Desiree bellowed.

Rayven took three giant steps and snatched the bouquet of flowers from Jazmin's grasp. She shook them at Sean and asked, "You give her these? What for, Sean? Why are you giving Jazmin flowers on Mother's Day? Are you...don't tell me you're ...?"

Rayven's voice trailed as she got lost in thought. She was rewinding time and replaying different scenes in her head. Her tear filled eyes connected with Sean's, reading the answer to the

4

question she had in her head. Her posture became heavy as the realization hit her.

"It's not what you think," Sean tried to explain.

Surprising everyone, Rayven started whacking Sean with the bouquet of flowers.

Jah found it amusing, "Damn! She fucking that nigga up!"

Before Jazmin could tell him to be quiet, Rayven turned on her and started attacking her. They formed into a ball of mangled bodies, taking jabs at one another and pulling hair. Desiree tried to break it up but her efforts were to no avail. It seemed like it went on forever but it was only seconds before Jah ended up pulling Jazmin in one direction and Sean had Rayven by her waist pulling her in the opposite direction.

Jazmin was incensed. Her once neatly groomed hair was pulled out of its place and all about her head. With an infuriated scowl on her face she looked like a mad woman.

"Get out!" Jazmin shouted. "Everybody, get the fuck outta my house!"

"You did this!" Desiree spat at her with an accusatory tone. She jabbed her finger in her direction for emphasis, "You! Do you realize how this looks, Jazz? You fucked my best friend's husband! Is he Genesis' father?"

"Get out of my house!" Jazmin repeated.

"You're trifling and you're every bit as guilty as he is!" Desiree chastised.

Sean continued to half carry and half drag a furious Rayven as she shouted out obscenities and insults.

"You fat bitch! You're nothing but a big, fat whore! Can't get a man of your own so you wanna fuck mine!"

"I hope you're happy with—"

Angry with tears streaming down her face, Jazmin shouted at her sister, "Just get out! Get outta my house, Dez, and tend to your *best friend*!"

Before turning to leave, Desiree said, "Daddy's going to be so disappointed in you."

Jazmin turned to straighten the picture frame on the wall that had tilted during the commotion.

Jah began to speak, "You know this was gon' happen sooner or—"

"And you're still here because?" Jazmin asked him smartly turning towards him. "Please leave, Jah."

6

"I didn't do a goddamn thing to you!" he argued.

"You didn't have to open your big mouth either!" Jazmin spat.

Jah looked at her as if she had lost her mind. "What the fuck did I say? I didn't tell that girl her husband was fucking you!"

"You basically implied it."

"What the fuck, Jazmin! You wanna keep this shit going? You wanna keep fuckin' that nigga or something?"

She let out a frustrated sigh. "It doesn't matter if I do or don't. All you had to do in all of this was shut the fuck up!"

This was the second time Jazmin talked crazy to him and Jah wasn't feeling it. He called himself coming over bearing gifts to bring some happiness to her day, but of course he had to be reminded he wasn't enough for her.

"Man, fuck this shit," he said under his breath. He brushed past her and headed towards the front. Before heading out of the door he turned back around and demanded, "Give me my shit back."

"What shit?" Jazmin asked.

"Around yo' mothafuckin neck."

7

"Hello?" the grouchy female's voice answered.

"You at home?"

"I'm at my mama's. Nigga, you know it's Mother's Day, right?"

"Yeah, I know, but I wanna see you. Can I come over later?"

"You okay, Sean?"

He sighed heavily, "Not really. Some shit just happened and I just need to clear my head."

"And you wanna come hang out with me?" she asked sarcastically. "How cute. Your wife don't wanna be bothered with your ass now?"

"You know what... Nevermind," he said.

She laughed, "I'm just fucking with you. Let me make sure ain't nobody tryna come by. I'll let you know."

"Okay, I'll see you later."

"Bye bae."

———

When Jazmin entered her parent's house, she felt like all eyes were on her. She felt naked and exposed. She knew Desiree had been running her mouth. Not wanting to deal with what her father would say, Jazmin gathered Genesis, her things, and headed out to her vehicle.

"Jazmin!" Paul called out as he descended the porch steps.

She stopped and turned to face her father. "What is it, Daddy?"

"What's going on? What is Dez talking about?"

"What did she say?"

"Something about you being a homewrecker. Is everything good with you and Jah?"

Jazmin shook her head. She said softly, "But I'll be okay."

"I guess I'll have to talk to him," Paul said. Noting the distressed and saddened look on Jazmin's face, he said, "I can't have nothing happening to my baby."

"Daddy, I'm alright. And you don't have to intervene. Jah is just Jah. But did Dez tell you anything else?"

"She mentioned something about Sean and Rayven but wouldn't say much. But she's upset with you."

"She'll be alright. But I'm gonna head on home."

"Okay. Call me if you need me. I'll handle whatever I need to handle."

Jazmin laughed lightly. "Get back in the house, old man."

Paul gave his daughter a hug before heading back.

Once in the car, Jazmin called Tanya.

"Hey girl! What's up?" Tanya answered.

"What are you doing?" Jazmin asked trying to mask her emotions.

"Nothing; at home chillin' with Tyriq."

"You didn't go visit your mama?"

"I gave that bitch a card with some money in it. I don't need to be in her face," Tanya chuckled.

"You're awful, Tanya," Jazmin said shaking her head.

"Did you go see your mama?"

"Yeah, me and Desiree went earlier today and took her some fresh flowers," she answered. The thought of visiting her mother's grave made her think of Jah's mother. *Damn*, she thought. He probably was having a rough day as it was and then she probably added to it by yelling at him like she did.

"Are you okay? You don't sound too happy."

"I'm not."

"Is it your mama?"

"No."

"What did Jah do to you?"

"I'll tell you exactly what he did. He gave Rayven the impression that me and Sean had something going on."

There was silence on the other end. Jazmin knew Tanya was trying to process what she had just said.

Tanya finally spoke but with question. "Oh-kay...Now why would Jah do something like that?"

"Jah is an ass, that's why."

"But what you're saying isn't making sense...Unless...Do you and Sean got something going on?"

Jazmin answered with a heavy sigh.

"Bitch!" Tanya hollered. It actually startled Jazmin. She continued with excitement mixed with disbelief, "You've been fucking, Sean?"

"Tanya, look... before I say anything what I don't need is for someone to pass judgment on me. I have no one else to talk to about this and you're my closest friend," Jazmin said. She found herself getting emotional.

"She-she, Jazmin ain't thinking 'bout no other nigga except that dumb ass mothafuckin' Sean. Fuck her."

"Did she say that?"

"She got mad; she ain't have to tell me."

"What about the baby? Did you tell her about that?"

Jah grew silent in thought. So many things whirled in his head about *"the baby"* situation. At this point with how Jazmin was making him feel, he was beginning to wonder if it was even a point in telling her anything.

"I didn't get a chance cause stupid ass showed up," he said. He added, "But fuck it, I ain't even gon' tell her."

"Why not?" Sheena asked.

"It ain't gon' make much of a difference."

"But what about Genesis?"

"What about her?"

"How are you gonna handle that? I know you're not just gonna walk away from her."

"That ain't what I wanna do but Jazmin ain't gon' make it easy for me to stick around."

Sheena wagged her finger and smiled, "Again, you don't know that. Give her a minute and let her clear her head."

Jah's phone rang. He looked down at it and frowned, but decided to answer it anyway. "The fuck you want?"

"Checking to see if you were coming over tonight," Erica said.

"Why? You gotta let yo' other nigga know it's safe to come over?" Jah asked.

"C'mon, Jah. We already been through this. I ain't messing with no other dudes."

"Whatever," he mumbled. "Is that all you want?"

"Are you coming over?" she asked again.

"If I do, it'll be later," he answered. At that moment, he had Nivea on his mind.

"Okay," she said. "Just call me and let me know you're on your way."

"Bet," he said and hung up. He looked at Sheena and asked, "When dude next door 'posed to be coming back?"

"You talking about Nivea's husband?" Sheena asked for clarification.

"Ain't that nigga locked up?"

"Yeah, but I think she told Aunt Georgia that he was getting out in the next—" she paused and gave Jah a look of suspicion. She shook her head, "Don't even think about it, Jah. Leave that lady alone."

Jah laughed. "I ain't done shit…yet."

"Jah!"

Chapter 2

Everybody wanted to talk to Jazmin and she really wasn't in the mood. She had shut everybody out by turning off her phone. It had been two days since the incident and she was starting to feel the heaviest about it.

Maybe it was the shame and guilt, but she didn't feel like facing anyone just yet. Desiree called her several times and left voicemail messages that she was not eager to listen to. Phyllis and her father called too. She did accept a call from Tanya the day before, but she rejected Cassie's call. She was sure everyone in their circle knew what was going on.

Genesis lay on her back, moving her arms and kicking every so often. Jazmin could tell she was annoyed because she had the hiccups. She chuckled at Genesis' frown. She didn't think she would have such a mean, fussy baby, but Genesis was always mad.

"Do you miss, Jah?" Jazmin asked Genesis. She replied with a hiccup.

As her doorbell rang, Jazmin said, "Well, he's an asshole and I don't miss him."

She got up to see who was at the door. She was sure it was her father coming by to check on her. She looked out of the peephole to discover that it was someone she was pleasantly surprised to see. She swung the door open and practically jumped in Lamar's arms.

"Okay, I wasn't expecting this," he said.

"What are you doing here?" she asked excitedly. She ushered him inside and shut the door behind him. She took in the sight of him from his head to his shoes. Lamar was an ex of hers from a couple of years before. And he was still just as fine as ever. Lamar was poised and polish. He carried himself with an air of confidence. With his dark complexion, good looks, and suave behavior, he could have just about any woman he laid eyes on. He reminded her so much of actor D.B. Woodside, the guy that played Malcolm in the sitcom *Single Ladies*. When he and Jazmin started dating she just knew he was the one. And temporarily he was the one. He was the one that made her stop thinking about Sean so damn much. But for whatever reason, Lamar wasn't ready for the next step in their relationship. Jazmin wanted more than the dates and sex. She wanted to be exclusively his and him exclusively hers. But he didn't want to go in that direction. They ended up mutually walking away from the relationship although it was something Jazmin didn't want.

"Where have you been?" she asked.

"Well, my job sent me across seas to help head up a new research division over there," he said.

"Still with Nissan?"

He nodded.

"That must have been nice. Where they send you?"

"Japan, and it was nice," he said. He looked around, "I see things haven't really changed."

She smiled coyly. "Well, actually, they have. Follow me."

She led him towards her den and pointed to Genesis on her play mat. "I got a lil' person to take care of now."

"A baby?" Lamar asked with surprise as he walked over to study Genesis. With a bright charming smile, he said, "Jazz had a baby?"

"Her name is Genesis," she said.

"She's gonna be pretty just like her mama," he told her. He directed his attention back to Jazmin and poked his bottom lip out in a pout. "So you couldn't wait?"

Jazmin was confused, "What do you mean, wait?"

"I always thought you would wait on me."

She said, "I tried. But when we went our separate ways, you never expressed anything like that."

"I know. I just had this feeling that you and I were soulmates but I needed to get some things out of my system before settling down. I was hoping you would have waited for me."

Jazmin looked down at Genesis. "Well, this was something that just happened. She wasn't intentional. I'm not even with her father."

"Since when did you not practice safe sex?" he asked with amusement.

"I know right," she rolled her eyes. "Shame on me."

"Is he a part of her life?"

Jazmin gave it some thought. "She sees him."

"Oh," Lamar nodded knowingly. "Can I sit down?"

"Oh sure. Can I get you anything?" she asked.

26

"What do you have to drink?"

As Jazmin headed into the kitchen to fix Lamar something to drink she heard what seemed like the sound of music near her house. Instantly she thought of Jah. She hoped like hell he wasn't popping up at her house.

As she poured Lamar's drink she heard the chime of her alarm signifying a door had been opened. With the drink in hand, she stepped around the kitchen corner and looked down the hallway at Jah approaching.

"Who the fuck pretty boy car is that out there?" Jah asked.

"Why are you here?" Jazmin asked with aggravation.

Jah looked at the drink in her hand and took it from her. "Damn, you must've knew a nigga was coming."

Jazmin's mouth dropped open as she watched him drink from the glass.

Lamar cleared his throat to make his presence known.

Jah looked over at him and slowly lowered the glass. "Who the fuck this nigga?"

us though. I could have shown homeboy something."

"No need in behaving like him. It's not you," she said. She didn't want Lamar to stay away. Perhaps if he had never left, she wouldn't have gotten so caught up in Sean which led her to having dealings with Jah. Lamar was ideal for her and she knew he was what she needed to get over both Jah and Sean.

"Take my number," she told him. He took out his phone and programmed her number in it.

"With a guy like him; you be careful," Lamar said before backing out of the driveway.

Jazmin watched him take off down the street before she turned back to her house. She dreaded facing Jah.

Going back in the house, she didn't find Jah nor Genesis in the den where she had left them. She called out, "Jah?"

When he didn't respond, she went upstairs to Genesis' room first. He was gathering some of her things himself while Genesis lay peacefully in her crib, slowly dozing off.

"What are you doing?" Jazmin asked.

"What the fuck it look like?" Jah snapped.

"You're not keeping her that long."

"How you gon' tell me how long I can keep my daughter?"

"She ain't your child; that's how!" Jazmin replied smartly.

"I don't see no other niggas around here giving a damn about her," he said. Then he thought about it. He stood up and looked at her. "Unless, you tryna get that black mufucka to be her new daddy. Where the fuck he come from any fuckin' way? I know his big ass wasn't driving that lil' bitty ass car."

"He's an ex," she said. "And I'm not trying to get any daddies for Genesis. Her father knows who he is."

"I don't want no other niggas around my baby," Jah said with finality.

"Whatever, Jah," she said dismissively. "Just hurry up and leave."

"You heard what the fuck I said," he said angrily. "And that mothafucka gay any gotdamn way. Big ass nigga driving that lil' sissy ass car."

"Gay? Yeah right!" she said and turned on her heels to leave.

33

Jah dropped what he was doing and followed behind her. "What the fuck that's 'posed to mean?"

"He ain't gay," Jazmin said smugly. She watched Jah out of the corner of her eye as he walked upon her. "Go on, Jah!"

"So I guess you finna start fuckin' him too?"

She frowned up at him, "So what if I do?"

"Damn, for real, Juicy? That's how you doing me?" he asked with disappointment.

Jazmin wasn't sure if his dejection was genuine or not but it was something in the way he said it along with the sadness in his eyes that did something to her. But she stood her ground with him.

"How am I doing you, Jah?" she asked.

He shook his head, "Nothing man."

"No, how am I doing you?" she asked again. He went to turn away from her but she stopped him. "How do you want me to do you, Jah? The same way you do me? Being disrespectful? Is that how you want me to do you?"

"I don't disrespect you and getcho' hands off me," he told her.

"Do you think I enjoy being cussed at all the time? Or what about how you jerked me by my arm down there in front of Lamar?" she pointed out. "Would you let me do that to you in front of other people?"

"You ain't crazy," he said matter of factly.

"My point exactly!" she exclaimed. "If you wouldn't want me doing that to you then why should it be okay for you to do that to me?"

"You ain't never had a problem with the way I talked. This nigga show up and now yo' ass got a fuckin' problem."

Jazmin opened her mouth to respond but thought against it. It would be pointless.

"Do you wanna be with me, Juicy?" he asked.

Jazmin was taken aback by the direct question. She gave it some thought and suddenly felt uncomfortable. Before answering she decided that Jah was standing too close to her. "Can you move away?"

"Answer the question first."

"No, I don't," she stated firmly. She went on to explain, "I thought I did at first because of everything I was going through with Sean. But then the other day made me realize you're only in this to get under Sean's skin. You get a kick out of all this mess and aggravating people. Just like when we were younger."

Jah made a scoffing noise as he backed away from her. "You're right. Just like when we were younger. I said nice shit to you all the fuckin' time just to aggravate you. I sho' in the fuck did. And I been being a daddy to *our* baby just to get under Sean's skin. I brought you flowers and a mothafuckin' nine thousand dollar necklace 'cause you the mothafuckin' mama to my child just to get under every fuckin' body's skin!"

Before Jazmin could say anything, Jah dug in his deep front pockets of his jeans and threw the Tiffany & Co. box at her.

"Fuck you, Jazmin!" he spat angrily.

"Jah!" she called after him. "I didn't mean to make you mad."

"Leave me the fuck alone," he said over his shoulder as he hurried downstairs.

"So you're not gonna get Genni now?" she asked hurrying behind him.

"I'll send my auntie to get her. But right now, I need to get the fuck away from yo' retarded, stupid ass 'fore I say some shit I might regret."

Jazmin followed him to the front door. He was slamming the door closed by the time she caught up with him. She opened the door just to watch him jump in his car and back out like a madman.

She shook her head and mumbled, "Idiot."

———

After two days of no communication, Rayven decided to return home. Much to her surprise, Sean was there. He was on his phone when she walked into the bedroom they shared. When he saw her, he quickly got off the phone and hopped out of bed.

"Hey baby," he greeted. He tried to embrace her but she stepped back.

"Who were you on the phone with?" she asked. "Was it one of your girlfriends? Was it Jazmin?"

"No, that was my cousin," he explained. He went for her again. "I'm glad you're home."

"Yeah, whatever," she said dryly. She walked over to their chest of drawers to retrieve some fresh nightwear.

"Baby, I think we need to talk about the other day," he said.

"Sean, I'm not really in the mood," she said.

"But we need to so we can get our marriage back on track."

"You've had two days to come up with a perfect lie," she said, her voice laced with despondency. She sat down at the foot of their bed and looked up at him with tired eyes, "Go ahead. Give me what you got."

"Don't do that," Sean said. He sat down next to her. "We've been together way too long to just throw it all away over a misunderstanding."

"A misunderstanding?" she let out a wry laugh.

"It was all a misunderstanding. What you heard was completely misconstrued," he explained.

"Sean, I specifically heard you say to Jazmin, 'I ain't losing you to him'. How can that be misconstrued?"

"Okay you were upstairs when you heard it," he argued.

"No I was coming down the stairs when I heard that. Hearing that another male was downstairs is what made me and Desi come downstairs in the first place. Never would have thought it would have been you!" she said widening her eyes.

"Yes, but you know how I feel about Desi and Jazz. We all grew up together and I always considered them like the sisters I never had. You know that. Me, Rock, Damien, Ed...we all treat Desi and Jazz like sisters and we're there for them whenever they need a male around...like a brotherly figure of course."

"Continue," she said listlessly.

"Did Jazz tell y'all about catching Jah in her house with another woman?"

"No, but what that gotta do with you and Jazz?"

"I'm getting to it. You were aware that she put Jah out, right?"

"Yeah, but she never really disclosed why she did it."

"Well, she called me crying one day and told me everything. Naturally, I got mad so Jah and I had some words. That's why he and I haven't been really talking. I told her he—"

"Wait. What did he do?" Rayven asked.

"He was fucking another woman in her house while baby Genesis was right there," Sean said incredulously for dramatics.

"Are you making all of this up?" she asked looking at him with suspicion.

"It was Erica. Don't believe me, ask Erica if she was caught in Jazz's house."

Rayven turned up her nose in disgust. "That skank?"

Sean nodded. He was eager to tell the rest of his lie. "So to cheer her up, I got her some flowers for her first mother's day. I didn't know Jah would actually come through for her. But you didn't hear me say, 'I ain't losing you to him'; you heard me say, 'I ain't letting you go with him'."

Rayven gave it some thought. What Sean was telling her could possibly be the truth. "So why did Jah act that way? He was acting like there was something between y'all."

"Seriously? Do you think Jah would be okay with me, his homeboy messing with his baby mama? Don't you think he would have been more livid than what he was? That was just his way of fuckin' with me."

"But when I asked Jazz she didn't tell me anything like she was struggling with telling the truth."

"Of course she's gonna struggle to tell you the truth when there was nothing to actually tell," he said. Then he sighed, "Well, I mean, Jazz has always had a crush on me. Everybody knew that. And there was a time she tried to come on to me, but I was with you already. I rejected her as nice as I could and let her know she was nothing but a little sister to me. She and I haven't had any issues since then."

"So, Genesis is not your child?"

Sean laughed in disbelief. "No! My child? The only child I have hasn't been born yet. And he's right there." He pointed to her stomach.

Rayven smiled feeling somewhat relieved. The story he told was plausible and for the moment she would give him the benefit of the doubt.

She said, "Well, I know Genesis can't be anybody's but Jah's. She looks just like him."

Sean faked a laugh. He was tired of everyone saying that. If Genesis looked so much like Jah that she could possibly be his, Sean wanted to know how and when Jah and Jazmin were together.

41

"So does this mean we're good?" Sean asked.

Rayven caught her bottom lip between her teeth and nodded with a smile.

Sean smiled and moved in to finally embrace his wife. Relief fell over him but now he had to get to the bottom of Genesis' paternity.

Chapter 3

Jazmin sulked on her sofa. This was not how she was supposed to be feeling. She always fought not to lose, but she had always been destined to lose from the beginning. It was wrong to lust after another woman's husband. She couldn't take back the affair with Sean, she couldn't take back Genesis, and she couldn't take back what she had given of herself to Jah. That's what she was the most angriest about. Jah had been an unnecessary factor to the equation. She should have kept him a non-factor. But no! She had to open her legs and catch feelings.

As much as she tried to not think about him, she found herself wondering about him. She missed having him in the house. She missed fussing at him about his trail of trash he left behind. She missed laughing at him. And she definitely missed sharing the same bed with him.

Her phone rang and she jumped. She quickly went for it to see it was Desiree calling.

Reluctantly, she answered, "Hello?"

"How are you?" Desiree asked in an even tone.

"Okay," Jazmin mumbled.

"You don't sound okay," she said.

"I'm okay. What do you want?"

"Jazz, you know me and Damien's anniversary trip is approaching. I know you've paid already or whatever, but since Rayven will be there with Sean, do you still want to come?"

"They're still going?"

"I suggested that she still come and try to work things out with Sean. It might be good for them."

"So basically you're calling me not to ask if I'm coming, but to see if I would not come."

"Something like that."

Sarcastically Jazmin said cheerfully, "You're a bitch and I don't like you."

Desiree returned with, "And so are you but you're a bitch that sleep with people's husbands."

"Who said I slept with Sean?" Jazmin asked. She now didn't want no one knowing about her affair with Sean. No matter what, she was the one that was going to be looked at as the villain, the homewrecker, the hoe, and just plain wrong.

"But you want to. Sean said you came onto him before but he had to put you in your place. He

44

said that he see you as his little sister and that's why he was at your house Sunday. He was giving you flowers for Mother's Day but he was upset seeing Jah there. Is it true that Jah had some other girl in your house having sex with her with Genesis right there? Sean said you called him crying about it. That's why he was telling you Sunday that he wasn't letting you be with Jah."

Jazmin couldn't help but to giggle. "Wait a minute. So what all did you and Rayven hear?"

"This isn't funny, Jazmin. None of it is. My best friend has been depressed these last couple of days because of this. It's not good for her or the baby. Why would you let her think that you and Sean had something going on? And Jah...well, I don't expect much from him."

"You're stupid and so is your friend. Goodbye Desiree," Jazmin said and ended the call.

Just then, the doorbell rang. She gathered her purse and powered off her television. She headed for the front door. Before opening the door she made sure she was smiling.

Expecting to see Lamar, Jazmin's smile faded at the sight of Sean.

"What do you want?" she asked dryly.

45

Sean smiled, "To see you. You're looking pretty today. Going somewhere?"

"I'm going out so if you don't mind, can you leave before he gets here," she said. She wanted to see how Sean would react.

"With Jah?" Sean inquired.

"No, not with Jah," she said.

Sean's eyebrow furrowed with confusion. "With who?"

"Don't worry about it, Sean," she sighed. She tried to shut the door but Sean prevented it from closing.

"What do you mean, don't worry about it?" Sean asked pushing the door further so he could step in the house.

Jazmin stepped back. She rolled her eyes. Now she had to deal with idiot number two.

"So you've met someone already? You're replacing me?" Sean asked.

"I can't replace what I never had," Jazmin answered sarcastically.

"Where's Genesis?"

"She's with Jah," she answered.

"With Jah?"

46

"No, you're not about to act all brand new, Sean. You know that man treat Genesis way better than you. His aunt and sister like having her around. When would Genesis ever get to meet your mother?"

"But that's not his damn child, Jazz!" Sean bellowed angrily.

"Look! How about you go to Ms. Georgia's house and go get your daughter and keep her for a few days with you and Rayven?" Jazmin got back just as loud with him.

Frowning, Sean gave Jazmin and intense glare, "Is Genesis my baby?"

Confused, Jazmin asked, "What do you mean?"

"She don't look nothing like me," he stated.

"That's because she looks like me."

"No...No, she doesn't," he said. With his head cocked to the side he asked, "Did you and Jah fuck last year, Jazmin?"

"No!" she said offended. "Why would you think that?"

"Because, Genesis look just like that nigga. Everybody keep saying it!" he said piercing her with an angry stare. "What the fuck, Jazmin! You've been

47

fucking that nigga all this time! That's his fucking baby!"

"I hadn't been fucking Jah!" she said in her defense. She grew angry. "So now you wanna disown Genesis altogether?"

"If she isn't—"

He was interrupted by the sound of the doorbell. Jazmin cut her eyes at Sean as she answered the door. Her scowl was immediately lifted by the sight of Lamar.

Sean's lip went up in a snarl. "This nigga?"

Lamar nodded an acknowledgment in Sean's direction. "What's up, Sean?"

Sean ignored him. He looked at Jazmin, "So, is this what you've been doing?"

Jazmin rolled her eyes as hard as she could and let out a frustrated breath. "I need to lock up my house so I can go on my date."

"I ain't finished talking to you, Jazz," Sean said as he made his way out the door.

Lamar chuckled and said, "I see you have all of the guys arguing over you now."

"Sean's a nobody," Jazmin said.

"Isn't he married to your sister's friend?"

She nodded but didn't bother to disclose the true nature of her relationship with Sean. She didn't want Lamar looking down on her and passing judgment.

She followed Lamar onto the porch. She locked up and they headed to Lamar's little red Nissan GT-R sports car. She snickered to herself as she thought back to what Jah said about Lamar and his car.

"What's funny?" Lamar asked. A smile formed on his face as he opened the passenger door for her to get in.

"Nothing," she said still giggling. God, she hated Jah, but she loved him at the same time.

———

Georgia walked in Sheena's bedroom holding Genesis close to her. She looked at the brother and sister pair laying lazily in bed. Jah was up under Sheena and it reminded Georgia of how he used to be as a kid always under her sister Marilyn.

"Jah," Georgia said. "I got a question."

"No to whatever it is," Jah mumbled.

Georgia sat on the edge of the bed beside Jah. "I'm serious now."

Sheena tapped Jah on his forehead with the remote control. "She's serious, Jah."

"What is it, Auntie?" Jah asked.

"Now...lemme get this straight," Georgia started. "According to what you told me and Sheena, this baby 'posed to be Sean's baby. But the more I look at her, I see nothing but you. Now how is that?"

Sheena started giggling. "Yeah Jabari, how is that?"

Wearing a goofy smile Jah shrugged, "Ion'eenkno Auntie."

"Boy, you know," Georgia said cutting her eyes at him playfully. "Why didn't you just say there was a possibility that you could be the father?"

Sheena mumbled something under her breath and had a fit of giggles.

"What Sheena?" Georgia asked.

"Nothing," Sheena said with a cough. "I'm not in this."

Georgia looked back at her nephew. "Y'all being all secretive and shit. She must know something that nobody else know."

"I ain't sayin' nothing," Sheena said. She tried to stifle a cough.

"Okay, I might be Genesis biological daddy," Jah admitted.

"Is Jazmin gonna get a DNA test to confirm it?" Then a thought occurred to her. "Damn, how does Sean feel about you and Jazmin fucking?"

"Auntie!" Sheena scorned.

"Well, it is what it is, Sheena," Georgia said. She looked back at Jah for an answer. She frowned and asked, "Do Sean even know you and Jazmin was together."

"Jazmin don't know either," Sheena giggled.

Jah hushed Sheena. "Man, be quiet. I ain't gon' tell yo' ass shit else."

"What? What she mean by that, Jah?" Georgia asked.

"Nothing," he said. "She sleepy. Go to sleep She-she."

There was a light knock on the outside of the bedroom. Brian appeared in the doorway. Sheena's eyes lit up.

"Hey! You made it," Sheena beamed.

Brian smiled. He acknowledged Georgia and Jah, "Hey Mrs. Wilson. Hey Jah."

Georgia smiled at him pleasantly. "Hey Brian. Are you hungry?"

"Auntie, you ain't gotta feed people every time they come over here," Sheena teased.

Jah eased out of bed. "I guess it's my time to go. C'mon Auntie and getcho nosey ass on up outta here."

"I am Jah, and you finna tell me 'bout this baby," Georgia said.

Jah greeted Brian with a very confusing handshake that Brian wasn't able to keep up with, but he got the shoulder bump right.

"Lil' nigga, you aight?" Jah asked looking down at him.

Brian nodded.

Georgia laughed on their way out of Sheena's room. "Jah, stop calling that man lil' nigga. He gets so beet red when you do."

"That lil' white mothafucka is a nigga," Jah said. "He aight with me though. If Sheena like them lil' scrawny ass white dudes then that's what she like, long as he continue to make her smile like she just did, I ain't fucked up with it."

Once in the upstairs den off from the kitchen, Georgia whispered, "You know he had proposed to her but she turned him down. It was right when she first got diagnosed. She tried pushing him away but he still came around. Eventually she said fuck it and let the man come around."

"He must really love my sister then," Jah said. He reached out for Genesis, "Give me my baby."

"No, let me hold her til' you get ready to leave," Georgia said.

"You gon' spoil her ass, Auntie!" Jah said. "And when her little big ass wanna be held I'ma bring her straight over here to you."

"Auntie won't mind," Georgia said as she bounced and swayed with Genesis. She smiled and said, "Your mama would be spoiling the hell out of her if she was here. So it's my duty to do it for her."

"Yeah, whatever," Jah waved off.

"Jah, if this your baby then how come you ain't tryna make things work with Jazmin? I know she love you and you love her. Y'all need to get it together."

"That's Jazmin," he said. "I wanted to be with her but she ain't tryna be with me. Now she going on dates and shit with this tall, bald headed, black ass nigga."

"And it's your fault if she get away from you," Georgia said.

"How the hell it's my fault?" Jah asked. "I can't make her love me no matter what the fuck I do. She dumb as hell and I ain't finna keep wasting all my time and energy to get her to give my ass a chance."

"But you just don't walk away on love like that."

"Yeah, yeah," he said waving her off. "Give me my damn baby; how 'bout that."

Georgia pouted. She said to Genesis, "Your daddy is big ol' meanie."

Genesis responded with a grunt as her face turned a shade of red. It was followed by flatulence.

"Aw hell naw!" Jah said. He headed out the den and said over his shoulder, "You got that Auntie. That sounded explosive!"

———

Going out with Lamar reminded her of why she had been so taken with him in the first place. He was charming and a true gentleman that knew how to conduct himself.

"So, when will you be returning to work?" he asked.

They had just finished up dinner and Jazmin was now slowly eating on her chocolate cake. "I guess in the next couple of weeks," she answered.

Lamar looked down at her cake and said, "Are you planning to eat that whole thing?"

"That's my intentions," she said with a smile. "You want some?"

He shook his head. Then with a seductive smile he said, "The only thing sweet I want to eat is you."

Jazmin blushed and looked away from his stare.

"Don't indulge too much in sweets. You'll never lose the weight you've picked up with the pregnancy," he said.

His statement bit Jazmin, but instead of being offended, she had to agree with him. She pushed the cake aside. "You're right. I do need to watch my weight."

"We'll get it off. Didn't we do it before?"

She smiled remembering how Lamar would work out with her and keep up with everything she ate. Some days it was annoying and aggravating. Other days she appreciated him motivating her like he did. She replied, "Yeah."

"So, are you excited about returning to work soon?"

"Kinda. I like the idea of being a stay at home mother too," she said.

"If your husband could provide all of the household financial needs, would you be a stay at home mother?"

She half shrugged. "I don't know. Maybe."

"How about more kids?"

"I do want another child one day but I really wanna do it right. I want the husband and not some baby daddy."

Lamar chuckled as he sipped his drink. Placing the glass back down he said, "Tell me about that situation. So you've got two men who are clearly a little...off; that claim to be the father of your baby?"

"Well, they both think they're the legitimate father of Genesis. One biologically and one in his head. And honestly, I'd rather the biological one step up and be the father full time."

"So where would that leave the other man?"

"He can be Uncle," she snickered.

"You slept with these men at the same time?"

"You mean in the same bed at the same time? No!"

Lamar chuckled, "Not in that way. I'm asking if you were seeing these two men at the same time."

"Oh no."

"So you definitely know who the real father of the baby is?"

Jazmin didn't have to think about it. She answered, "Yes! I know when I conceived and everything. I'm one hundred percent sure of who my baby's father is."

"So if you were to go on Maury," he laughed.

Jazmin laughed and answered before he could ask. "I would not be one of those women that'd be running backstage and crying."

"Okay," he shot her a look.

"Do you still plan to have kids?" she asked.

"Actually, I do," he said with a nod.

She noticed he got a little uneasy and averted his eyes to the table.

"That's why I came looking for you. But I wasn't aware you had just given birth to your own baby," he said.

Jazmin was confused. "I don't understand."

"I want a baby and I want you to have it for me," he said.

Jazmin laughed but was still uncertain of what Lamar was asking. "You want us to have a baby?"

He nodded.

"But you just came back into my life."

"I understand that but we have history. I know you. You're pretty and you're smart and you come from a nice hard working family."

"So when did you all of a sudden want kids? Did you just wake up out of the blue and decide to come find me so we can have kids right away?"

"No," he said. "It was something I've always wanted with you. I mentioned it to you before."

"Yeah, but I didn't think you were serious because you weren't ready to take our relationship to the next level," she said.

"I wasn't and that's why I backed away," he chuckled. "I just didn't think you would up and have a baby during the separation."

"Separation? That's what that was?" She asked mockingly.

"Jazz, I thought it was understood that we were just taking a breather from one another."

"No, a breather is a few months, Lamar. You were gone for quite a while...like two years."

"I didn't think you would have moved on so quickly."

"What was I supposed to do? Be miserable and lonely waiting on you?" she asked. Then she thought about it. The past sixteen months she had been miserable and lonely anyway.

"No, I know you had a right to live, Jazz. And it was my mistake for not thinking that another man would love to be with you."

That warmed her a little. Of all her exes, Lamar was one of the ones that praised her on how she looked even though she never embraced the skin she was in.

She said, "Well, can this be something I think about."

"Sure. You don't have to give me an answer now. Take as long as you like...well within reason."

"And in the meantime we can continue to see each other and see how things go," she added.

He nodded with a smile. "Of course."

———

Jah had been ignoring Jazmin all night long. He kept sending her straight to voicemail. He knew

59

she didn't want anything. She just wanted to know what Genesis was doing every five minutes.

As a matter of fact, he was trying to get rid of his feelings for Jazmin. Hell, he was wasting his time trying to get her to see him as someone she could be with. He had been trying since he was a teenager and she was a preteen. And every time he thought he had won her over, she would remind him once again that he wasn't good enough.

Jah actually thought after he took her virginity she would have given him more thought. She didn't bother to contact him at all. And when Jah finally did come back around, she just looked down her nose at him and kept going with not so much as a *"Hey Jah"*. And he had to admit, that hurt his feelings. He was done with Jazmin.

"Was that enough?"

Erica's sweet voice snapped him out of his thoughts. He placed his phone down and smiled at her, "Yeah. That was more than enough, baby."

"Was it good?" she asked coyly.

"I woulda told you if it wasn't," he told her.

Erica reached out for his empty plate. Taking it from him she asked, "Is there anything else I can get you?"

Jah gave her a wicked smile, "You know what you can do."

She blushed and shook her head. "What am I gonna do with you, Jah?"

"Same mothafuckin' thing you always do. Fuck you mean? Shiiid," he said with a chuckle. "Yo' kids sleep?"

Jah hadn't been with Erica in over a month. Initially, he didn't want to complicate things between them after he put it out there that he wanted to be with Jazmin. He told Erica he simply wanted to be friends. But then she announced that she was pregnant. He told her he would be there for her and that's what he was doing. She had been begging him to come over, so he finally caved in, being that things were pretty dead between him and Jazmin.

"They are but let me go check on them real quick," she said.

Jah admired the shape of her ass as she walked away. She certainly wasn't Juicy at all. Erica had a slimmer build but she had a nice body on her. But it was something about the way Juicy walked; one ass cheek was going this way while the other

61

tried keeping up. It was just ass everywhere. And Jah loved it.

He chuckled to himself as he thought of Jazmin. Even the way their houses were kept was different. Erica was more of a free spirit with less structure. The kids had toys everywhere in every room. She had baskets of clothes that needed to be folded; they were scattered about. And she kept dirty dishes in her sink. It didn't bother Jah too much, but he realized he did miss the atmosphere Juicy offered, although he got on her nerves.

When his phone rang and it displayed Jazmin was calling again, he decided to answer it. "Yeah?"

"What are you doing?" Jazmin asked. He couldn't really read her voice. She was using a very flat tone.

"Are you finna have one of them mothafuckin' breakdowns again? 'Cause I can't help yo' ass this time."

"Why have you been ignoring my calls? Anything could have been going on. I could be sick."

"But you ain't. So what the fuck you want?"

"Why are you talking to me like this, Jah?" she asked.

"What the fuck you want?" he repeated.

"What's Genni doing?"

"Do you see what time it is?"

"Yeah, Jah," she exhaled in frustration.

"She sleep, Jazmin," he told her even though he wasn't sure if that was true or not. He had left Genesis in his aunt's care for a couple of hours.

"Can I hear her?"

"What the fuck you think you gon hear? She don't snore."

"Why are you so mean?" she asked.

"Why the fuck you calling me? You ain't been calling me. Leave me and my baby alone. You can get on her nerves when I bring her lil' big ass back."

"Wait," she said. "I'm bored."

"Bored? Call that gay mothafucka in that lil' ass sissy ass car."

"He just left," she said.

That hit a nerve. Yes, he just told her to call on gay boy, but he didn't actually want the nigga around her.

"He had to leave or you asked his ass to leave?"

"He left on his own," she said.

"You know what, Jazmin?" he laughed. "Big niggas like him driving in little ass red cars like that are either gay or they are cheaters with a whole mothafuckin' family on the side."

"Jah, shut up," she said. "You don't know shit. You always talking."

"Okay. Why that nigga leave? Did he try to put his dick in yo' pussy before he left?"

Jazmin sucked her teeth loud. "You know what, Jah? Every man don't have to be like you, okay?"

"And what the fuck that's 'posed to mean?"

"You put your dick in all kinds of pussies, all the time," she said.

Jah was thrown by her vocabulary. Jazmin would never say *"dick"* or *"pussy"* out loud. He laughed a little, "Juicy, you okay?"

"Yeah, why you ask me that?"

"How old are you?"

"Twenty-eight...No, no, no...twenty-nine. Hold on...," she said. He could hear her trying to count on her fingers.

Jah laughed, "Juicy, yo' ass must be drunk!"

"I'm not—who's drunk?" she asked.

"How much you had to drink?"

"Nothing," she answered.

"Nothing?" he laughed. "Man, take yo' ass to sleep. I'll talk to you in the morning."

"Jah!" she hollered. "Guess what Sean had the nerves to ask me the other day — no, today?"

"What, Juicy?" Jah asked patiently. Erica returned to the living room and plopped down on the sofa beside him. He cut his eyes at her with detest. She was dead wrong but he would address her after his call with Jazmin.

"Sean asked me if me and you had fucked last year. He thinks Genesis is really your baby."

Jah feigned surprise with obvious phoniness, "Whaaaaat?"

"I know!" Jazmin giggled. She stopped laughing. "We didn't though, did we?"

"Juicy, get yo' drunk ass off my phone," he said as Erica got back up with an obvious attitude and went to the kitchen.

"Jah!" Jazmin called out before he could hang up.

"What!" he snapped. Erica walked back in the living room and headed back to the sofa where he was. He stopped Erica from plopping down beside him. Instead, he got up. He said into the phone,

"How the fuck you not gon' know you ain't fucked somebody? What type shit is that, Juicy?"

Erica looked at him with confusion.

"I know right?" Jazmin laughed.

"Hold on, Juicy," Jah told Jazmin. Even though he told her to hold on she was still rambling on.

"What are you doing? You 'bout to leave?" Erica asked.

Angrily Jah asked, "Are you on your mothafuckin' period?"

Erica looked stunned. She shook her head and said, "No. I'm pregnant Jah, remember?"

"Yo ass ain't pregnant smelling like that. You smell like you on yo' period and you ain't change yo' mothafuckin' pad or tampon, or whatever the fuck it is you put up in yo' pussy."

Erica was completely embarrassed but it angered her more. "Why would you say some shit like that?"

"Because, when yo' black ass plopped down beside me on the couch I smelled you. Either yo' ass stink or it's yo' pussy. Regardless, you need to sit yo' ass in some water."

"You so fuckin' rude and disrespectful," she rolled her eyes.

"How am I being disrespectful? Yo' pussy rude and yo' ass disrespectful. Like goddamn, every time you sit down you don't smell that shit yo' mothafuckin self? What the fuck? Who you been fuckin', Erica?" Jah asked infuriated. The faint sound of Jazmin's voice could still be heard as she continued to ramble on the phone.

"Nobody but you," she said.

"And the last time I fucked you was when my baby was born. That was over a mothafuckin' month ago. You didn't have these kind of problems then. Fix the shit; then holla at me and maybe I'll come through. Other than that, keep me updated on the baby," he said.

Erica was infuriated as she watched Jah exit her townhome. She slammed the door behind him. She found her phone and dialed Sean. Of course he didn't answer, so she left him a message: "So you ain't gonna call me back? Where the fuck are the antibiotics, dumb ass! You were supposed to pick them up for me today. And if I don't hear from you by tomorrow, I'ma call your wife and tell her everything! EVERYTHING!"

Chapter 4

Jazmin didn't want to wake up. She had too much to drink the night before. She didn't mean to overdo it but she still got carried away in her woes. A part of her had been confused by Lamar's proposition because she didn't know if she should take it as some type of agreement between two parties or if she should take it as him wanting something special with her. When he dropped her off the night before after their date and didn't bother to stay, it completely threw her off. Jazmin didn't know what to think.

So she was left feeling confused, horny, lonely, and bored. She giggled with her eyes closed thinking of her conversation with Jah the night before. Of all people to call while drunk she had to pick him. She couldn't even remember how it ended or when she had drifted off to sleep.

"What the hell you laughing about?"

Startled, Jazmin sat up and turned around in the direction of his voice. "What are you doing in here?"

"Making sure yo' ass aight," Jah answered.

68

Small waving fists and small baby noises caught her attention. Jazmin's face lit up with delight at the sight of Genesis on the bed beside Jah.

"My baby!" Jazmin squealed. She went to pick Genesis up but Jah pushed her back.

"Uh-uh," Jah said.

Jazmin looked at him puzzled. "What?"

"Go take a shower," he ordered.

Jazmin went to smell herself and realized she had on a nightshirt but with no panties.

"Smell yo' fingers," Jah told her.

"What?"

"Smell 'em," he told her.

"No," she said. She looked at him with suspicion. "What did I do?"

"Just smell 'em," he chuckled.

Cautiously she brought her fingers up to her nose. The smell was very familiar, rather arousing. She looked at him just as confused, "Did we have sex?"

"Naw," Jah said. "You had sex with yo'self."

"What?" she asked cracking a smile.

"Yo' ass was hot by the time I got here. You wanted to fuck but I didn't wanna do you like that. You got mad and told me you'll do it yo'self. So I said, okay. And I watched. And I got it on my phone," he laughed.

"Jah! Noooo! Why you let me do that?"

"I wasn't gonna stop yo' ass. Shit, I got me one too," he admitted.

Embarrassed, she dropped her head in her hands. Murmuring, she said, "Jah, please delete whatever you recorded."

"Uh-uh," he mumbled. "Now go take a shower so you can pick yo' baby up."

She lifted her head up and looked at him. "Is that all I did?"

"You really shouldn't drink to the point you can't remember shit, Juicy," he told her.

"I don't do it often," she said.

"It's still not good," he stated. He asked her, "What if you do that shit and you ain't got no mothafuckin' body around to make sure yo' drunk ass safe? What if you do it and there's a hundred mufuckas preying on yo' ass so they can take advantage of you?"

"But it ain't never happened," she said.

"No, it hasn't yet. But remember last year at that party Rock's brother had? Yo' ass was pretty fucked up then."

"Yeah, I know," she said a little dismayed. She remembered being angry with Sean. He had invited her to the party since none of the females from their circle was going to be in attendance. He promised her that she would have all of his undivided attention. After their first initial greet, he disappeared on her.

"Go take a shower so I can show you what you was doing last night," he chuckled.

Jazmin shook her head as she hopped out of the bed. "You're so not right, Jah!"

She quickly gathered her things and went to her bathroom. She made sure to lock the door because she didn't want Jah trying anything while she was taking a shower.

During her shower her mind wandered to Lamar. She remembered a time when she thought she would be his wife. It was funny because being in his presence didn't do anything to ignite those same feelings about him. *Perhaps it was because she wasn't totally over Sean? Or maybe it was because she wasn't being honest with her feelings about Jah? What was it about Jah that kept her from giving in?* She was afraid to give herself to him totally. She was afraid for him to love her, and vice versa.

71

Being more comfortable around him allowed her to walk out of the bathroom in just a towel wrapped around her body. She looked at Jah as she approached the bed. The top half of his dreads were pulled back away from his face into some intricate twisted style while the bottom half draped loosely over his shoulders. His chinstrap beard had been cut low and neatly trimmed along with the attached goatee. In the tank tee he was wearing, Jazmin noticed his arms had become a lot more defined and his tattooed covered forearms were snaked with corded veins. He was looking mighty good to Jazmin.

"What the fuck you lookin' at me like that for?" Jah frowned.

"No reason," she shook her head. She leaned over her bed to look at Genesis. She smiled as Genesis stopped gnawing on her fist to turn her head to find Jazmin.

"Hey Genni-boo," Jazmin said sweetly. "Mommy missed you."

Genesis cooed as if she could talk. Jazmin smooth her hair down. She then traced her delicate eyebrows. "You got them ol' bushy eyebrows like your daddy."

"Sean got bushy eyebrows?" Jah asked with feigned interest.

Jazmin looked up long enough to make eye contact with him as she nodded. "Yep, her daddy got bushy ass eyebrows."

"Hmmm...never noticed," Jah mumbled. He looked at Jazmin lovingly. He hated that his feelings for her were deep. He hated that he thought she was so beautiful. He hated that he wanted her badly. He hated that no matter what he did, she didn't want him.

Hesitantly, Jah said, "Ay, I'm sorry about the other day with ol' boy. I ain't tryna see you be with no other nigga. And I'm dead mothafuckin' serious."

"Why Jah? It ain't like we're together anyway," she pointed out.

"Juicy, shut the fuck up before you ruin this shit. I know we ain't together, but that's what the hell I was tryna talk to you about before Sean's retarded ass showed up. How come you don't fuckin' take me serious?"

Jazmin ignored him as she continued to coo and talk to Genesis. Jah got up from the bed and walked out of her view. She assumed he had went out of the room but when she felt his presence behind her, she immediately knew what he was up to.

"Jah, don't be playing—" she was saying as she tried to turn around to face him. He pushed her back around to face Genesis and pressed himself into her. She could feel the hardness of him pushing through his jeans and poking her in the ass. As bad as she wanted to, Jazmin couldn't let him do it. "Jah, we can't."

"Shut up. You don't wanna take me serious but I bet you take this mufuckin' dick serious," he told her as he began undoing his jeans to free himself.

"Jah—" she tried to object again as she twisted her body to try to look at him.

He pushed her back around.

"But Genni is right here and awake."

"Shut the fuck up and lemme put this dick in ya'. Genni don't know what the fuck going on except for how her mothafuckin' fingers taste."

"Jaaaaahhh!" She cried out when she felt him enter her. He didn't try to be gentle at all. It felt like he rammed all of his length inside her at once on the first stroke. He groaned as he held still enjoying the way her walls gripped him.

He stroked twice more and noticed how slippery wet she was. He had to look down at the sight of his dick going in and out her. He gripped her ass cheeks and kept them spread apart as he began to pound her, occasionally slowing his pace to look at how her pussy juices lathered his dick. She was so wet that it was running down her thighs, glistening his whole pubic area. It even made a wet squishy sound with each thrust.

Jah groaned, "Fuck!"

Genesis' coos gradually turned into cries. Jazmin covered her own mouth with one hand to stifle her cries and moans and tried to give Genesis her pacifier with the other. It worked for a few seconds until Jah gripped her by the waist and started putting a pounding on her.

"Jah baby," she cried out. She reached behind her to control how far he went in but Jah pushed her arm out of the way.

Genesis spit out the pacifier and listened intently as her mother cried out to the gods and cursed Jah.

"Put that ass in the air," Jah ordered.

75

Jazz made her upper body go as flat as she could while pushing up her lower half creating a deep dip in her back.

"Jus' like that," he praised her.

She could feel his grip on her tighten as his weight became heavier on her. He quickened the pace to turbo speed. Between Genesis, Jazmin, the sound of his thighs hitting the back of hers, and his own guttural noises, it had gotten pretty loud in the room.

Jazmin felt her climax building inside her. The faster he got, the closer it came. He didn't let up until he knew he got her to that point. And even then he kept going until she balanced on the edge of euphoric bliss. Once she tipped over, there was no turning back. She let out a piercing wale that turned into full blown crying. Her pussy walls convulsed uncontrollably as Jah continued to try to stroke through them.

"Please!" she cried as she tried to crawl away from under him.

"Be yo' ass still! Do you want me to stop?"

"No," she whimpered.

"Then shut the fuck up and stop moving!"

It was just too much for Jazmin to bear. "But…Jah…oh God…please…"

He ignored her as he slowed his pace but grinded deep inside her. He tried to kiss her on her shoulder and neck but she was too sensitive and her whole body jerked. Bearing his weight on her, he dug into her deep. He held her down in such a way that she couldn't escape, although she was begging to be free.

He spoke into her ear, "I'm finna cum in this pussy, my pussy. You hear me?"

Jazmin felt like she was being tortured because her ears were her most erogenous spots on her body. They were the most sensitive and with each word he spoke his lips grazed against them causing her to shiver beneath him. She tried to turn her head but he wouldn't let her move. He licked in her ear causing her to scream. It was too much.

"Juicy, I love you."

She couldn't explain why, but hearing Jah say those words to her made her start crying all over again. Hearing his succession of grunts signified he was emptying all he had inside her. She just lay there underneath him, trying to control her emotions.

Genesis suckled on her fist.

Out of breath and drenched in sweat, Jah said, "I think yo' baby hungry. And yo' ass trifling for fuckin' in front of yo' child."

———

Tanya scrunched up her nose in disapproval. "That doesn't say him. That look too preppie. Girl, I told you where we need to go. We need to go to them hood stores like *CitiTrends*, *Marty's* and *615*. That's if you still wanna get him something to wear."

Cassie said, "Or you can always go the cologne route. Get him some Gucci or Versace. Those smell good."

"I think he already has those," Jazmin said absently as she looked around the vast department store. "Maybe I can get him some shoes."

"Get him a watch," Tanya suggested.

Jazmin stopped pushing Genesis' stroller. "Y'all do know I gotta get him something for Father's Day next month so some of this stuff I ain't thinking about getting."

"Father's Day?" Tanya teased. "So is that what he is now. He's the pappy, Jazz?"

"Well, you know what I'm saying," Jazmin corrected.

"When is his birthday exactly?" Cassie asked.

"It's the Wednesday after Memorial Day," Jazmin answered.

"We'll be in the mountains then," Tanya said.

"Yeah," Jazmin said. "I've already ordered a cake for him too."

"I think somebody been hit by the love bug," Tanya teased.

"It ain't nothing wrong with that," Cassie said. "When her and Jah are cool, Jazz posses this glow about her and an extra bounce to her step."

"That's what happen when you getting good dick," Tanya said.

"Will you stop?" Jazmin playfully slapped Tanya on the arm. "I only got it once this past week."

"That was enough, shit. If it got you shopping for birthday gifts and talking about Father's Day, then it's some good D."

"Actually, I'm doing it because I'm nice and caring, and he's my friend."

Tanya rolled her eyes, "I'm so sick of y'all and this friend shit."

79

"Speaking of friends," Cassie said. "What's up with Lamar? I heard you hanging back out with that nigga. Where did he come from and where did he disappear to?"

"Bitch, I told you about Lamar," Tanya told Cassie.

"Did you?" Cassie asked.

"Yes dumbnut! You up there talking like you supposed to have just heard about it. You ain't good at acting, you know that?" Tanya fussed.

Cassie snickered, "Well, my bad. So Jazmin, what are you going to do about Lamar's ass?"

"Nothing," she said. "He's just a friend too, although he wants to have a baby."

"What?" both Cassie and Tanya asked in unison.

"You didn't tell me 'bout that," Tanya said.

"Cause I didn't think he was really serious," Jazmin said. A piece of merchandise caught her eye and she asked excitedly, "Why don't I buy Jah a man purse."

Tanya side eyed Jazmin. "And he gon' man purse that shit upside your head. Keep fucking with Jah if you want to."

Jazmin laughed at herself because she knew buying a man purse was an absurd notion.

As the ladies continued to peruse Nordstrom, Tanya asked, "So, is you gon' let Jah move back in?"

Jazmin frowned, "Well, he hasn't asked about it. As a matter of fact, I hadn't really heard from him since the other day which is weird. He's usually harassing me about Genesis."

"If he asks, are you gonna let him?" Cassie asked.

Jazmin shrugged. "I don't know."

"What about Lamar?" Tanya asked.

Jazmin shrugged again. "I simply don't know."

Tanya then asked in code, "But what about that other situation?"

Jazmin looked at Tanya and frowned. "I'm ending that."

Tanya smiled, "Good."

"What situation?" Cassie asked. "Y'all talking about shit I don't know nothing about. I wanna be in the loop."

"It's nothing, Cass," Jazmin said dismissively.

Cassie walked over to the row of glass cases that contained eye catching designer watches for men. "This is nice, Jazz."

Jazmin pushed the stroller over in Cassie's direction but halted when she caught a glimpse of someone she knew walking by the entrance of the store. *I know that wasn't who I think it was*, she thought.

Tanya answered her thought, "Wasn't that Sean?"

"Where?" Cassie asked looking up from the watches.

"Let's go mess with him," Tanya giggled. She took off in the direction where she saw him going.

Jazmin called out, "Leave him alone. He seemed in a rush."

Cassie wore a frown and followed Tanya. Jazmin blew air in annoyance. She didn't really care to see or talk to Sean. But with reluctance, she and Genesis followed her friends.

"Where he go?" Jazmin asked when she caught up with Tanya and Cassie.

"I think he's going to the food court," Tanya said.

Narrowing her eyes, Cassie said, "Let's just follow him and see what he's up to."

The three ladies and Genesis discreetly trailed Sean to exactly where Tanya assumed he was going. Keeping their distance, they watched with surprise as he met up with a female. The two greeted with a hug and sat down at a nearby table. They immediately got into a seemingly serious conversation. The female looked frustrated and troubled. It was obvious she was upset with him. He kept reaching across the table to hold her hand but she kept moving her hands away. Eventually, she allowed him to hold them, as he seemed to pour his heart out to her. She didn't want to hear what he was saying. He continued to talk to her and she nodded. They got up and they shared a hug before walking off together.

Tanya's mouth hung open, Cassie looked angered, and Jazmin didn't know what to think.

"What the fuck going on with that?" Tanya wondered out loud.

"That's what I wanna know," Cassie said.

Jazmin's face frowned with bafflement. "Why...I mean...what could those two be talking about without Damien and Rayven?"

Georgia smacked her lips loud. "Now you know he ain't gon' say nothing about you and Genni being over there."

Sure, Jazmin thought. This had been the first time she heard of Jah having his own place. She said, "Yeah, I know. But you know how Jah can be. But thank you Ms. Georgia. I'm not gonna keep you."

"Okay baby. Call me anytime. And kiss that lil' one for me."

"I will. Talk to you later," Jazmin said before ending the call. She quickly dialed another number.

"Hello?"

"What unit does Jah live in?" Jazmin asked.

"Well hello to you too, Jazz," Abe spoke sarcastically.

"Yeah, yeah, yeah. I know you're good. Tell Lovely I said hi and I know your kids are bad. Now, what unit Jah live in?"

"Why?"

"Cause I need to know."

"I ain't giving you that man's address. If he wanted you to know where he lived he would have told you," Abe said with amusement in his voice.

"C'mon Abe! I really desperately need to know where he lives."

"Depends on why you want to know."

"Really?"

"How's the baby?" he asked.

"She's good. She misses her daddy and that's why I need to know where Jah lives. Genesis told me to call," Jazmin snickered.

"Sure," he said unbelievingly. He asked, "So where is Sean?"

Jazmin was thrown because she didn't realize anyone knew about that. "I guess he's at home with his wife."

"Isn't Sean the baby's real daddy?"

Jazmin sighed with defeat. Instead of answering she said, "Look, Jah is ignoring me for some reason. I need to talk to him because I'm pregnant and it's his."

"Huh?"

"You heard me, Abe."

"You and Jah are really fucking?"

"Yes."

"Well damn! I thought it was supposed to just be an act. He ain't told me this shit. Wait until I see his ass…And he got you pregnant!"

Jazmin laughed. "So will you give me that address now?"

Twenty minutes later, Jazmin arrived at the condos where Jah resided. The elegance of the building didn't fit Jah at all. It made her wonder why he never disclosed to her that he had his own place. *And if he did have his own place, why did he need a place to stay all those weeks ago?* Maybe he had just moved in.

Carrying Genesis in her carrier, Jazmin made her way into the building. She checked in at the attendant's desk. He did what Jazmin was hoping he wouldn't do and called Jah's unit. There was no answer. The attendant called his unit again and still no answer. Just as the attendant was hanging up, the elevator opened and out walked Jah.

Jazmin smiled at the sight of him. When he looked in Jazmin's direction he did a quick double take.

As Jazmin opened her mouth to say something, an attractive lady walked right out of the elevator behind Jah. For a brief second Jazmin maintained hope that the lady wasn't with Jah.

"Oh, there's Mr. Bradford," the attendant said.

Jah was still looking at Jazmin as the woman he was with looped her arm around his. He watched

Jazmin's smile slowly fade and her shoulders drop. Her saddened eyes locked with his and said everything she needed to say.

Jazmin gripped the handle on Genesis' carrier and looked away. She smiled at the attendant and said, "Thanks." She began walking off towards the front entrance. Jah and the woman were headed in another direction of the building.

She tried to fight back tears and ignore the hurt and pain as she made her way to her car. She didn't understand what happened between her and Jah and maybe it wasn't for her to understand. But what Jazmin did know, was that she was tired of being mistreated by men.

"Jazmin," Jah called out to her. He had come out of the front entrance and was now following her.

Jazmin ignored him and continued her journey to her car.

"I know you mothafuckin' hear me," Jah said to her. He had closed the gap between them and was right behind her as she began putting Genesis in her car seat's base.

"You ain't gotta explain nothing to me," Jazmin said firmly.

"I know what the fuck I ain't gotta do," he said. "But I didn't come out here to explain shit. I wanna know how the fuck you know where to find me."

Jazmin closed the back door and opened the driver's side door preparing to hop in. She looked back at Jah, "It doesn't matter. Just pretend I was never here."

"What did you come here for?"

"To see you, Jah. I thought maybe you would want to see Genni. And I hadn't heard from you since you left my house Saturday. And you hadn't been answering any of my calls. But now I see why. But it's all good."

"It is all good. I ain't worried 'bout you or any mothafuckin' body else. And don't bring yo' ass back over here looking for me either," he said angrily.

"What did I do to you, Jah?" she asked returning the anger and frustration.

"I ain't got time for your lil' wishy washy, petty ass games," he said wearing his infamous scowl.

"What games? I thought we were good."

"Who the fuck told you to think that? You ain't finna keep on fuckin' with my feelings Jazmin. I said I was done trying with you. I don't even know why I took my ass to yo' house Friday night any fuckin' way. I set my own goddamn ass up for that. You do whatever the fuck you feel like doing whether it's with Sean bitch ass or that gay mothafucka driving that lil' ass red car."

"How have I played with your feelings, Jah?" she wanted to know.

He averted his eyes and just shook his head.

"So just like that; I don't matter to you anymore?" she asked.

"Go head on with this shit. You ain't gonna pull this shit with me. When I tried to show yo' stanky booty ass that you mattered, you pushed me the fuck away. So how the fuck it feel being on the other end of not giving a fuck?"

"I didn't push you away," she argued.

"After that lil' shit with Sean and Ray atcho house you told me to get out after I asked you to be my woman. I said 'okay, she got that shit'. I wasn't planning on talkin' to yo' ass no time soon. Then I go to yo house, you got another mothafucka over there. I asked yo' black ass if you wanted to be with me; you told me no. Then I knew I really needed to keep my goddamn distance from yo' ass. But then you call me drunk and shit so I went to yo' house to make sure you aight or whatever. When we had sex Jazmin, I told you I fuckin' love you and you never said it mothafuckin' back. As a matter of fact, you didn't really say shit to me afterwards. I get it now, Jazmin. You don't want me. It's cool. I'm done with tryna chase after your ungrateful, stupid ass. I'm done!"

Jazmin stood outside her car stunned as she watched Jah walk away from her. She started fiddling with the diamond heart pendant of her necklace as her emotions started to rattle. She didn't know if she should go after him or what. She thought about her pregnancy. Because he was the father, Jazmin felt like Jah should know but since he said all of what he just said, she was hesitant to even let him know.

Chapter 5

Thoughts of Jazmin and Genesis were nagging at Jah. He was so tempted to call her and tell her he didn't mean none of the things he had said to her the day before. But he was tired of feeling this way about Jazmin. He didn't want her to continue to have the hold she had over his heart. If he could just find the switch that would immediately turn off his feelings, it would be so much better.

"What are you over there thinking about?"

His eyes cut to Nivea and he stared at her for a minute. She was supposed to be his distraction but it wasn't working. This was his second time being intimate with her and although she was more experienced and confident in the bedroom, it didn't compare to being with his Juicy.

"Thinking 'bout you," he lied.

Nivea smiled and moved closer to him. "What about me?"

Damn, he thought. He shouldn't have lied. Now she wanted to engage in sweet talk. Ignoring her question, he got out of bed and started looking for his clothes. He said, "Ay, I'm finna head on back to my auntie house."

Disappointed, she asked, "You didn't plan to spend the night?"

He shook his head. "Hell naw. So yo' kids can see me over here like that? Then they gon' tell they mothafuckin' daddy when they see me at my auntie house, 'that's the man that was layin' with mama' and I know I'ma have to end up shootin' his ass."

"They won't know what we're doing," she argued.

"Bullshit. Kids be knowing," he said as he stepped into his boxers and jeans.

"Are you coming back soon?"

"I'll be back but I don't know when."

"Isn't your birthday next week?"

He had forgotten about his own upcoming birthday. He needed to get Jazmin out of his head. "Yeah, it is."

"You got anything planned for it?" she asked sweetly.

Jah sat back down on the edge of her bed so he could put his shoes on. "Naw, not really. I was supposed to go out of town with my fucked up friends. I don't think I wanna be around they mufuckin' asses. They a bunch of stupid, retarded ass, dumb ass people."

Nivea giggled. She lay on her side holding her head in her hand on her propped elbow. "Why do you talk about your friends that way?"

"It's the truth. But they know that's how I feel cause I say it to they mufuckin' face."

"So you're considering not going out of town?"

"I don't know," he mumbled. It would be nice to be in Jazmin's presence but hell, he was trying to get over her.

"Will it be the whole week? And where are y'all going?"

"We posed to go to Gatlinburg where they done rented one of them damn cabins. Don't know why the fuck they wanna be in the mountains to do some white people shit," he said then started laughing. "I hope one of 'em get mauled by a goddamn bear."

"That isn't nice, Jah," Nivea snickered. "I wouldn't mind going with you. I would love to spend your birthday with you."

"Don'tcho ass gotta work?" he asked.

"I can call off."

"The whole goddamn week? You finna get fuckin' fired."

Nivea laughed. This was one of the things she loved about Jah; he always kept her laughing. "I won't get fired because I'm the boss."

Jah turned to look at her and a smile eased across his face. The way she said that sounded sexy as fuck! "You're the boss?"

She smiled and nodded.

"So yo ass wanna come with me for real?" he asked.

"Yeah."

He smiled. "Aight."

"So when do we leave?"

"Tomorrow. Will you be ready?"

"Yep. How we getting there though?"

"The nigga whose anniversary it is renting some vans."

"Will there be enough room for me?"

"It should be," he answered and stood to his feet. He asked, "Ay, whatchu do with that other condom?"

She flipped over and looked on her side of the bed. She pinched the used prophylactic in between her thumb and forefinger and held it up.

"Here it is. What? You think I'm gonna do some slick shit?"

Jah took it from her. "I don't know. Gotta watch you hoes. Y'all be tryna set a nigga up."

Slightly offended, Nivea said, "Really Jah? So I'm a hoe?"

After going to her bathroom and flushing both used condoms down the toilet, Jah stepped back into her bedroom and said, "Aintchu married?"

"Yes but—"

"Then you a hoe," he chuckled. "Fuck you talkin' bout. You got a whole 'nother nigga stashed away in prison."

"Shut up, Jah," Nivea said rolling her eyes.

"Nigga, just be ready when I come knocking on yo' door tomorrow," he said. He headed out of her bedroom. "Come lock this door man."

If Sean were forced to get his shit together and choose a woman to settle with in a monogamous relationship, it would be Jazmin. Had he known she would have made him feel the way he felt for her, he would have given her a chance years ago. It probably would have prevented him from marrying Rayven. He loved Rayven, but compared to Jazmin her personality wasn't as appealing any longer. But Sean didn't feel like going through a divorce; and now that she was pregnant, he surely didn't want to be put on child support. He was catching hell with Erica trying to pay her already. Then there was Genesis. Jazmin hadn't demanded anything from him for their love child which further troubled Sean. He was suspecting that Jazmin wasn't being truthful about her and Jah.

He waited patiently on the porch for the door to be answered. When Sean went to press the bell again, the door swung open.

A frown immediately covered her face and she let out an annoyed breath. "Why are you here and what do you want?"

"Can I come in?"

Jazmin stepped aside to allow him in. She closed the door behind him, folded her arms over her chest, and stared at him.

Solemnly he asked, "How are you?"

"I'm good," she answered curtly.

"Where's Genni?"

"She's back there."

"Can I see her?"

Jazmin didn't respond. She simply headed back to the den with him following her.

Genesis was laying on her play mat on her stomach. She was moving about and trying to talk.

Sean picked her up and held her close. "She sure does have a lot of hair."

"Yep."

"She moves a lot like this all of the time?" He asked.

"She's very active and thinks she can talk," Jazmin said with a smile. "I think she cusses me out all day."

"That's not good," Sean said as he took a seat on the sofa.

Jazmin eyed him suspiciously as she sat in the love seat. "Why are you here? Last time you came by you were saying Genesis was Jah's baby."

"I know. I've just been a little stressed."

"Really? So how are things with you and Rayven?"

He thought carefully before answering. "We're alright, I guess." He looked down at Genesis and said, "I think it's time I started being a real father."

Jazmin folded her arms across her chest. "Really? How many times have you said that same phrase since she's been born?"

"Jazz, stop with the unnecessary comments. But since Ray is about to have my child I might as well get adjusted to having two."

"So what does that mean exactly?"

"It means, I need to have a relationship with my daughter," he said.

"Is that why you came over?"

"I came over to see both of you," he replied.

"Does Rayven know where you are?" she asked.

"Nope."

"Did you tell her the whole truth yet?"

"Nope."

"What are you gonna do?"

"What do you mean?"

"Are you gonna leave things the way they are between you and her or are you moving on? I mean, despite the lies you told her to cover up everything, I'm sure she has doubt."

He interrupted her, "She doesn't know anything really. She's made an assumption off of what Jah implied and our lack of an explanation at that moment."

Jazmin frowned. "What are you saying, Sean? You're gonna continue to lie and deny Genesis, huh?"

"I'm saying I still don't want her to know the truth just yet."

"Huh?" Jazmin was growing hot with aggravation. "So where does Genni fit in?"

"She doesn't have to know the real truth."

"Well what truth did you tell her, Sean?" Jazmin asked angrily.

"I've already told her that what she heard was misconstrued. I also told her that Jah thought the same thing and created the confusion."

"But it was implied that we were fucking, Sean!"

"No, not really."

"Sean," she started but blew out a frustrated breath. "So you wanna work out your marriage?"

Sean kept his eyes on Genesis and answered, "Yeah."

Jazmin let his response sink in. She was supposed to despise him right now but her heart felt crushed. She wanted him to want something with her and Genesis. She wanted Sean to love her so much that he couldn't see himself without her. She felt like a fool.

"What about us?" she asked. "We're completely done, right?"

"You have Jah now," he said.

"So you just giving me to him now?"

"It's what you wanted, Jazz," Sean said finally looking in her direction.

"I didn't want Jah; I wanted you!" she yelled. "You're the one that put Jah on me to keep yourself from being caught."

"I know, but you and him took the shit somewhere else," Sean spat.

"And you're sitting there acting like you have a lot of room to talk."

"Jazz, if you and I were together and it was supposed to be you and me, no other nigga should have been able to have you."

"But you were having Rayven the entire time," she argued.

"And you knew what that was. I was going to take care of it but you got impatient and jumped on the next nigga's dick."

"It was a mistake! I was lonely and he was here. You're the one that neglected me and Genni. Jah was here; he was here!"

"So where is he now?"

"Not here," she answered.

"No, where do he fit in all of this now?"

"Not here," she repeated.

Sean looked down at Genesis who was staring back at him. It was one of the first times she had ever remained peacefully quiet in his arms. Genesis was over a month old now and he could see a little bit of himself in her.

He asked, "What's up with you and Lamar?"

"Why do you care? You just gave me to Jah," Jazmin said smartly.

"Look, Jazmin, you're gonna have to choose. You can't have us all and I don't wanna share you with another man. Especially not with Jah. If you wanna still see what you and I can have, then you gotta cut Jah completely off. And with Lamar, go ahead and nip that in the bud too."

"Sean, I'm gonna do what I want to do. You sir don't have that power over me anymore. I don't—"

"I'm not trying to have power over you," he interrupted. He looked at her tenderly, "Jazz, I love you and I want things to go back to how they used to be."

"Oh being secretive and unclaimed?" she asked with sarcasm.

"Just until Ray have the baby," he told her.

"Why then?"

"I don't wanna leave her during her pregnancy."

Jazmin nodded. "Okay Sean. So in the meantime, you're just gonna be a daddy to Genni whenever you're in the mood."

"I'm gonna spend more time with her, Jazz."

"And I suppose you're gonna demand that I don't let her be around any other men, especially Jah."

"Would that be so hard to do?"

"Jah is Genesis' father," Jazmin stated blatantly.

Sean's face morphed into anger. "What the fuck does that mean?"

"It means the right man signed her birth certificate. I'm not gonna keep her away from Jah."

"Are you fucking serious right now, Jazz?"

"I'm dead serious. You wanna play games and set the rules, well, so will I."

"Who's playing games? This is real life shit that can't be handled overnight. You're on some bullshit with this Jazmin."

"How is Jah being Genesis' father hurting anything?" Jazmin wanted to know. "It's been working just fine so far."

"Fuck Jah," Sean spat. He got up and placed Genesis back on her play mat. "I gotta go."

"Wow! A whole twenty minutes. Genesis is really gonna get to know you with time like that," said Jazmin with cynicism.

Ignoring her he asked, "Are you still coming for Desiree and Damien's anniversary getaway?"

Jazmin was glad he brought her sister up. It reminded her of the mall incident. She asked, "Do you ever talk to my sister by herself?"

Confused he asked, "What are you talking about?"

"Like, do you meet with her without Damien or Rayven?" she boldly asked.

"No. Why would I?"

Jazmin scoffed. The fact that he lied reminded her that he was scum. Sean was the most selfish, low down, manipulative person she knew. She didn't want him but she knew he got a rise out of thinking that she wanted him. But Jazmin was going to hurt his feelings real soon. She wanted him to feel everything she had felt dealing with him and his empty promises.

––––––––––

After dropping Genesis off with Phyllis and her dad the following day, Jazmin headed over to Tanya's to pick her up. When she got there she wondered whose navy blue Tahoe was sitting in the driveway.

Not bothering to knock, Jazmin walked right on in Tanya's house. She always kept her door unlocked out of carelessness.

"Tanya!" Jazmin called out. She noted Tanya had her things together and they were sitting on the floor by her sofa.

"Jazmin! Is that you!" Tanya yelled from upstairs.

"Yeah! You ready?"

"Here I come!"

Jazmin took a seat and waited for Tanya to come down. When Tanya did come down the stairs, she wasn't alone.

Tanya was smiling. "We're ready."

Jazmin smiled awkwardly. She looked over at Tanya's company. "She's coming with you?"

Tanya nodded. She grabbed the red headed white woman by her arm and pulled her close. "Jazz, I'd like you to meet Sabrina. Sabrina, this is my best friend, Jazmin."

Sabrina stuck her hand out and smiled, "Nice to meet you. Tanya talks about you a lot."

Still feeling awkward and totally confused, Jazmin took her hand. "Nice to meet you too. I've never heard Tanya speak of you before."

Tanya explained, "That's because she and I just met. I showed up over Ricky's house one day and she was there. We hit it off and she sold me a whole bunch of weight loss shit. Girl, I done lost ten pounds. Can you tell?"

Jazmin giggled, "I guess I can kinda tell. So what are you selling, Sabrina?"

"I sell teas, detoxes, HCG liquid...I also sell Avon. If you're interested in any of it just let me know. Here's a business card," Sabrina said enthusiastically.

Jazmin took the card and studied it. Out of curiosity she asked, "You were selling this stuff to Ricky?"

Tanya answered, "Naw, she Ricky girlfriend. He acted like he was scared to say she was his girlfriend at first. I was like nigga, it ain't shit wrong being down with the swirl."

Jazmin said, "I didn't know Ricky had a girlfriend."

"I didn't either 'cause you know all them niggas is hoes," Tanya said. She looked over at Sabrina sheepishly, "Sorry I said that bout'cho man."

Sabrina chuckled lightly, "Oh no, you're fine. Ricky and I are just starting out. It's not that serious yet."

"And I had to cuss Sean's ass out. That nigga don't never be at home with the wife he so call supposed to love," Tanya said with a roll of the eyes.

"Sean's been spending a lot of time at Ricky's lately," Jazmin said more as a thought.

Sabrina asked, "So will Sean and his wife be on this trip?"

"They should be," Jazmin said.

Tanya asked with concern, "Are you gon' be fine with that?"

Jazmin's eyes shifted to Sabrina. She didn't want this stranger speculating on anything. Tanya got the hint and didn't say anything else.

Jazmin smiled, "Well Sabrina, welcome to our little circle of dysfunctional friends."

"Awesome," Sabrina said cheerfully.

After leaving Tanya's, Jazmin headed towards Lamar's apartments. After witnessing Jah with his female friend and the things he said to her, Jazmin reached out to Lamar to invite him along on the trip. She needed the distraction and the company.

Lamar greeted Jazmin with a kiss when he got in the car. "Thanks again for inviting me. I need this before I go back to work next Monday."

"Shit, I think we all do," Tanya said from the backseat.

Lamar turned around to greet both Tanya and Sabrina. "Hey Tanya. How are you ladies doing?" He looked at Sabrina and said, "I don't believe I've met you. I'm Lamar, Jazmin's future husband."

Jazmin blushed and side eyed him. He looked over at her and gave her a quick wink.

"Aw! Isn't that sweet?" Sabrina crooned. "When is the wedding?"

Jazmin answered, "Sabrina, don't listen to him. There is no wedding."

"Oh, but you two look like you fit," Sabrina said.

"I'm trying to tell her that," Lamar said playfully.

Jazmin peeked at Tanya through her rear view mirror. "Tanya, you promise to be on your best behavior?"

"I'ma be good," Tanya stated. She looked back at Jazmin's reflection. "You make sure you be good."

———

Upon arriving at Damien and Desiree's, Jah saw that just about everyone was already there. Looking at the people that were there, he had a mind to abort the trip and go back home. The only people he was glad were coming along was Nivea of course, Rock, Rock's brother Ricky, and Ed. Damien was cool but he was still a cornball like Sean.

Avoiding Sean, Jah helped the other guys load all of the cargo on both vans. Sean was one of his least favorite people at the moment. Sean was a bitch. And apparently he had told Rayven some bullshit to smooth things over between them. Jah couldn't understand what it was about that nigga that made women so stupid.

"Well, here comes Jazz and Tanya," Rock said eyeing Jazmin's jeep. "We can go now 'cause that's everybody."

Jah looked over as Jazmin's car made its way around the back of the house where the others had parked. "Who the fuck was that in the car with her?"

"Hell, I don't know," Rock answered.

When Jah saw Lamar carrying his belongings alongside Jazmin, he groaned with annoyance. "This big gay ass nigga. She would bring his ass."

"Aw shit. Ain't that her ex?" Ed whispered. "Y'all ain't together no more, Jah?"

"We never was," he answered.

Lamar walked towards where they were standing at the back of the vans. "Here you go."

"Nigga, you better put that shit in there yourself," Rock said wearing a frown. "We ain't no damn baggage handlers."

111

Jah snickered, "Rock, yo' ass stupid."

Lamar chose to overlook Rock's and Jah's petty behavior and loaded his things as well as Jazmin's in the back of the van.

Jazmin peeked her head out of the van on the left, "Lamar, we're in this one."

When she moved out of sight and Lamar had made his way onboard, Tanya was heading towards them with her stuff. When Jah's eyes landed on the person behind her, his mouth dropped open. "What the fuck?"

Rock, Ricky and Ed turned around to see what Jah was talking about.

"Oh shit!" Ricky muttered under his breath.

Rock asked, "Ain't that ol' girl that..."

"What the fuck y'all looking at?" Tanya snapped playfully. She shoved her stuff into Ed. "Here, put that shit up."

Sabrina looked at the men and blinked a few times without saying anything.

Sean walked over oblivious to what was going on. "Let's get ready to head out. Ed, you still driving—"

And it was at this moment that Jah knew Sean realized he was fucked up. Seeing Sabrina threw Sean off and he was at a loss for words. She simply smiled at him wickedly and followed Tanya onboard the left van.

"I'm driving this one," Rock pointed to the left van to break the awkwardness.

Ed headed over to the right one. "I guess I'm driving this one."

Sean asked in a lowered voice, "How and why is she here?"

"She was with Jazmin and Tanya," Rock answered.

"Jazmin?" Sean asked puzzled.

"Remember we pretended she was Ricky's girl that day Tanya came over," Rock reminded him.

"People don't believe that this a small world," Jah said mockingly. He gave Sean a taunting grin. "I think you gon' like this lil' getaway. You got all yo' womens."

Sean cut his eyes at Jah and headed to the right van. Jah couldn't help but laugh at Sean's dilemma.

———

113

Jazmin hated that Jah had to sit right in front of her with his lady friend Nivea. She didn't want to look at them the entire way to their destination.

Initially, when Jazmin got on the van she didn't know who Nivea was. She didn't even bother asking who she was there with; Jazmin just started speaking to her. Nivea was well put together; a lot classier than Jazmin thought Jah would be interested in. She was light skinned and had thick box braids that she had in a balled bun atop her head. She was pretty with a sweet smile, but the way she conducted herself, Jazmin guessed her to be older than she was. She was nowhere near the heavy side as Jah claimed he liked. Nivea was average size, maybe as size eight. And one thing Jazmin was sure of was that Nivea was not the same woman she saw Jah with at his condo.

Jah turned around and looked at her. He asked, "Where Genni? Who she with?"

"She's with my daddy and Phyllis," Jazmin answered.

Jah looked at Nivea and asked while nodding his head in Jazmin's direction, "You know that's my baby mama right?"

114

Nivea frowned and looked back at Jazmin, "This is her or are you playing?"

Jazmin answered, "He's playing. He's delusional. He has a baby on the way by a girl named Erica."

"Oooh!" Tanya hollered. "Jazmin, now why you put that man's business out there like that?"

Ricky laughed, "Y'all petty than a mufucka."

Jah cut his eyes at Jazmin. "Whatchu call yoself doing? Niv already know 'bout that any mothafuckin' way."

"So y'all not together no more?" Michelle asked. "And Jah, why you get that ol' skanky girl pregnant?"

"Shit happens," Jah replied bluntly.

Cassie asked, "So this not weird to y'all?"

"Fuck Jazmin," Jah mumbled under his breath.

"Fuck you too, Jah," Jazmin shot back.

Lamar pat Jazmin on her thigh. "Don't entertain it, bae."

"I really hope I don't regret coming on this trip," Jazmin said more to herself.

Jah said, "Yeah, me too."

Chapter 6

Three and a half hours later they arrived at the rented seven bedroom, three level chalet. It was really nice. Even though it was large, it still provided them a nice, cozy, charming and country mountain atmosphere.

Jazmin was glad she and Lamar chose an upper level bedroom. There was a whole floor between them, separating them from Jah and Nivea. Jah's jerkiness was turned up to the max and he was irking her nerves already.

"Are you okay?" Lamar asked.

She nodded.

He stepped to her and wrapped his arms around her in a comforting way. "Don't worry about that ass of a baby daddy you have. We'll just keep our distance. Besides, isn't this about Desiree and Damien's anniversary?"

Jazmin rolled her eyes as she pulled away from his hold. "It's supposed to be. The heifa didn't want me here."

"And why is that?" asked Lamar.

"Because her friend and her friend's husband are having issues," Jazmin replied as she removed articles of clothing from her suitcase.

"Rayven and Sean?" Lamar's eyebrow raised with his inquiry. Not understanding, Lamar asked, "Why does their issues have anything to do with you?"

Jazmin's mouth open to half explain but Lamar narrowed his eyes at her. He asked, "Does it have to do with why he was at your house that day?"

"Like I said then; Sean's a nobody," Jazmin responded as she put her things into the bedroom's closet.

Lamar mumbled under his breath, "I hope that's true."

Jazmin turned away from the closet. "I'm gonna step out for some air."

Lamar offered her a sweet smile. "Okay. As soon as Im done here, I'll join you."

Once she left out of the bedroom, Jazmin headed downstairs to the main floor. Cassie and Michelle's room was in visible sight with the door open. Jazmin saw that Tanya, Sabrina, and Rock were in there socializing as well.

Standing at the doorway, Jazmin asked, "What's going on in here?"

"Girl, Rock tryna get me to go in the room with Ed," Michelle stated with her nose turned up.

Confused, Jazmin asked, "Why would he want that? I thought you two were talking."

Rock grimaced with disgust, "I don't want her nasty ass."

Tanya and Cassie started laughing. Michelle rolled her eyes and twisted her lips up. "Nigga, if I was to give you this pussy you would take it."

Rock shook his head. "Uhm...no I wouldn't either." He chuckled and nodded his head towards the prescription bottle that had spilled out of her purse and onto her bed. "What's them pills for?" He gave her a menacing look. "I bet I know."

Michelle seemed to flush with a quick second of embarrassment as she reached for the bottle; however Sabrina scooped it up before Michelle could get to it.

Reading the bottle, Sabrina said, "Doxycycline."

Angered, Michelle snatched the bottle from Sabrina. "Give me my shit!"

Sabrina laughed in a taunting manner, "You should have just gotten the shot. It works just as good."

"Wait a minute," Cassie chuckled. She wore a puzzled look. "What the fuck going on here? Y'all know each other or something?"

"Nothing is going on and I don't know her white ass," Michelle mumbled as she tucked her prescription bottle away in her purse. She cut her eyes at Sabrina and said, "People just nosey as fuck."

Sabrina seemed unfazed by Michelle's anger which struck Jazmin as odd. Dismissing it for the moment, Jazmin turned around to walk away from their mess only to bump into another mess.

Frowning, Jazmin snapped, "Did you have to be so close?"

Jah sucked his teeth and dismissed her, "Man, ain't nobody tryna get close up on yo' mufuckin' ass. I came looking for Rock and yo' ass just in the way."

Jazmin rolled her eyes releasing a frustrated breath. "Just get outta my way."

"You get the fuck outta my way," Jah shot back.

Tanya walked out of the bedroom shaking her head. "Why don't y'all just kiss and make up?"

Smirking, Jazmin said, "The only man I want to kiss and make up with is upstairs."

Watching her walk away, Jah said, "That nigga ain't tryna kiss and make up shit with his gay ass. I seen the way he was looking at Rock's booty."

Frowning, Rock went after Jah, "Man, fuck you Jah! Go head on with that bullshit!"

Jazmin just shook her head as she tried to block out Rock and Jah's silliness. But it did give her reason to give it some thought. Since Lamar had been coming around not once had he tried to sleep with her; yet he wanted a baby. *How did he suppose that would happen if they never slept with each other?* But then again, how could she get pregnant on top of another pregnancy anyway?

As the three ladies enjoyed the views of nature from the main deck, Jazmin tuned Sabrina and Tanya out as her mind wondered on her dilemma. *What would happen if she didn't bother telling Jah she was pregnant with his baby? How would he act if he was aware of the baby?* He was so stubborn! She knew he would be insistent on being there for her which was a good thing; however, where would that leave things between her and Lamar?

While several of the others made a trip to the grocery store and with Rayven napping, Sean took the opportunity to approach Sabrina. He caught up with her at the bar on the lower level. She had been engaged in a conversation with Cassie and Ed.

Sean casually took a seat beside Sabrina. Cassie narrowed her eyes at him but he ignored her.

"Why the fuck are you here?" Sean bluntly asked Sabrina.

She laughed with amusement. "I was invited by my friend. Is there a problem?"

"Yes, it's a goddamn problem," he hissed angrily. "Why do you feel like it's okay to come around me and my friends; especially around my wife?"

"First of all Sean, I wasn't aware that I would be around you on this trip. Tanya asked me if I would like to join her. And since I'm supposed to be seeing Ricky, I thought it would make sense to accept the offer."

"Since when have you and Tanya become such good friends?"

"Since I saw it as a way to be closer to you," Sabrina said wickedly as she removed herself from the bar.

Sean shot daggers in Sabrina's back as she walked away. He turned around and a pair of cold eyes were staring back at him.

"What?" he asked with annoyance.

"You just keep on digging bigger holes for yourself, huh?" Cassie asked with disappointment.

"Shut up, Cass. I don't wanna hear it," he mumbled.

"You need to," she shot back. "You just don't give a fuck about poor lil' Ray do you?"

"It's none of your business," he said firmly.

"Maybe it isn't," she reasoned. "But what kind of friend would I be if I sat back and knew all your dirty lil' secrets and didn't expose you?"

An obnoxious smirk spread across Sean's face. "Because if you expose me, then you have to expose yourself."

"And I ain't even messed up with that," Cassie returned. She stared him in the eyes without waver. "Now who should I tell first? Ray, Jazz, or Jah?"

"Jah?" Sean screwed his face up with confusion.

Cassie chuckled victoriously. "Erica?"

The two of them were so enthralled with their back and forward threats that they forgot Ed was listening the entire time.

"What the fuck that mean?" Ed asked looking between the two.

Cassie nodded towards Sean, "Let him tell you."

"There's nothing to tell," Sean replied.

"What about Erica?" Ed inquired.

Cassie grunted a laugh as she poured herself another drink.

"You're a bitch, you know that?" Sean asked cuttingly.

"And you're a dog ass snake," Cassie countered.

"You're just mad because I won't fuck with you anymore," Sean said.

"Anymore?" Ed asked with raised eyebrows.

Cassie grimaced, "Do you know how long ago that was?"

"It doesn't matter. You've been trying to get this dick ever since," Sean taunted.

"Boy bye!" Cassie dismissed. "That lil' shit! The only women that want that don't know better."

Ed leaned over the bar's counter and asked, "You fucking Jah's girl?"

"No man," Sean lied glaring at Cassie.

Cassie started giggling as she sipped her drink. She looked over at Sean's scowl and burst into laughter. She said, "This is gonna be real good."

———

As they perused the aisles of the local grocery store, Jazmin wondered why it took seven people to get the job done. Of all people to take a trip to the store with, why Jah had to volunteer his ass. *Why didn't he stay back at the cabin with his lady friend?*

Pushing the grocery cart, Jazmin caught up with her sister. Desiree seemed to be studying the contents of a frozen food item but Jazmin sensed something was troubling Desiree. Since before they left for the trip, Desiree seemed distant and quiet. She wasn't even bossing Damien around which was unusual.

"Hey, what is that?" Jazmin asked cheerfully.

Desiree broke from her trance and glanced back at her sister. "Nothing."

Jazmin watched as Desiree carelessly tossed the item into the cart. She asked, "Are you okay?"

"I'm fine," Desiree mumbled as she continued to slowly move down the aisle of frozen goods.

"Are you still mad with me?"

Desiree looked back and Jazmin and offered her a small, soft smile and shook her head. "No. Why would I be?"

"Well, the way you were snapping off on me when you thought I had been sleeping with Sean; I assumed you were still mad at me. Especially when you tried to get me not to come."

"I'm over it now. I got my own problems to be concerned with than worrying about protecting Ray's feelings."

Jazmin thought back to the mall visit. She asked, "What kind of problems are those?"

"Don't wanna really talk about it," Desiree said as she opened one of the freezer doors.

"I'm here whenever you wanna talk," Jazmin offered.

Desiree paused and gave Jazmin a sneaky grin. "Actually, I do want to talk. What's up with you and Jah? And where did Lamar come from?"

"Me and Jah are obviously over. And Lamar showed up right after that lil incident at my house. I'm so glad he did too," Jazmin explained.

"But Jah gave you that and flowers," Desiree said pointing to the diamond heart necklace Jazmin was wearing.

"It wasn't a romantic gesture," Jazmin said as she subconsciously began fiddling with the pendant. "He got it for me for Mother's Day. That's all."

"That says more than just Mother's Day. So you're not willing to forgive him and work things out?"

"For having Erica in my house? Yeah, I forgave him for that," Jazmin stated with a dismissive wave of her hand. She sounded sad as she said, "But he moved on."

Showing concern, Desiree stepped closer to Jazmin. "You love him, huh?"

Jazmin frowned as if she was insulted. "No!"

Desiree chuckled. "Stop being so pigheaded, Jazz. There's nothing wrong with loving Jah. But the more you stay in denial, the further away he will get from you."

Jazmin softened as her sister's words touched her. She then realized her grasp on the diamond hear pendant had tightened. She released the pendant and sighed, "I think it's too late anyway. Besides, he got Erica pregnant, he has this Nivea chick, and not to mention I saw him with another female a few days ago. Did you know this dude had a condo this whole time?"

Desiree was about to speak but a few of the others were making their way down the aisle. Instead, Desiree said, "Well speak of the devil himself."

Jazmin turned around to look at Jah. She wanted to admire his looks but she quickly grew annoyed as he began removing items from the cart.

"What are you doing?" Jazmin asked.

"Ain't nobody eating this shit," he said as he tossed a bag of hotwings back into the freezer.

"That don't even belong there," Jazmin stated.

"Jah, what are you doing?" Desiree asked. "Damien eat those."

"We gon' make our own," Jah said matter of factly.

Desiree was amused. She grinned, "So you know how to cook, Jah?"

"Ask yo' sister," he said looking over at Jazmin.

Michelle came over to the cart and placed two buckets of ice cream inside.

"I don't eat that generic ice cream," Desiree said turning up her nose.

"Well get your own!" Michelle snapped.

Jazmin noticed a small container of Talenti Caramel Cookie Crunch gelato in the cart. "Oooh! I want some of that."

"That's yours," Jah told her. "I figured yo' greedy ass would want it."

Jazmin didn't try to hide the smile that grew wide across her face. "Aw! You're such a sweetie, Jah!"

Jah cut his eyes at her and walked away.

Jazmin's smile faded as she watched him get further away down the aisle. Desiree's words earlier echoed in her head. She abandon the cart and the others to go after Jah.

"What the fuck you following me for?" Jah asked without looking back.

"How did you know it was me?" she asked as she tried to keep up with him.

He stopped at the end of the aisle before heading down the next one. He looked Jazmin over, his eyes lingering more on the fullness of her breasts that jiggled with her every movement. "I know how you smell."

"So you're saying I stink?"

He shook his head and looked away from her with frustration.

She asked, "What's your problem? You've been a jerk towards me all day. But then you pick out one of my favorite ice creams like some type of truce offering."

"A truce offering?" he asked with annoyance. "Man, Jazmin, get the fuck on."

"Jah, stop being so mean to me. We're gonna be under the same roof again for seven days. Can we at least be cordial to one another?"

Jah watched as an overweight person on one of the motorized shopping carts exited the aisle behind Jazmin. "You betta move the fuck out the way before yo' ass get ran the fuck over."

Jazmin stepped closer to Jah to allow the person more room to pass. She looked up at him and immediately felt intoxicated by his scent. He looked down at her and if she didn't know any better she would think his eyes were closed because of his long lashes. That was another thing that Genni possessed; the extremely long lashes.

Not entertaining the thought, Jazmin asked, "So, are you and Nivea serious?"

"I ain't finna discuss that with you in no damn grocery store," Jah said.

"All you have to do is answer yes or no."

Jah returned with a question of his own, "You and gay dude serious?"

"Stop calling him gay!"

"Okay, he's fuckin' bisexual. Is that better?"

"Jah, I wouldn't have brought Lamar on this trip if you hadn't talked all crazy to me that night."

"I ain't talking 'bout this shit right now," he said as he stepped around her to go down the other aisle. However, he was almost hit by another person on a motorized shopping cart.

"Goddammit! These mothafuckas and these mothafuckin' hubberounds!" Jah yelled.

Jazmin cracked up with laughter. "It's Hoveround!"

"Whatever the fuck they is!" Jah said angrily. "They need to get the fuck out the goddamn way!"

"Stop it!" Jazmin laughed. She grabbed Jah by his arm and pulled him away from the appalled old lady. Just looking at the lady's face, had Jazmin crying with laughter.

Chapter 7

The following morning, Jazmin awoke rather frustrated and annoyed. *How does a grown ass, abled body man lay in the bed with a woman during a peaceful getaway and don't want to have sex?* Something wasn't adding up with Lamar. She was beginning to think that Jah could possibly be right about him being gay.

"Where are you going?" Lamar asked. He was still lying in bed.

"About to take a walk," Jazmin said with an attitude as she slipped on her black and white tribal capri leggings.

"That's a good idea," he yawned. He looked at her and said, "Your legs could use some toning."

Jazmin paused to give him a death stare. She simply rolled her eyes and continued with putting her running shoes on.

Lamar sniffed the air. "Somebody's cooking breakfast."

Jazmin ignored him and make her way out of the room. She headed down the stairs and for some reason she expected to see Jah in the kitchen cooking breakfast but it was Tanya, Cassie and Rock.

"You hungry?" Tanya called out to her.

Jazmin continued to the front door. "I'll get some when I come back."

"Where you going?" Cassie asked.

"Just a quick walk," she replied as she exited.

Jazmin took a minute to decide which direction she wanted to go. She didn't plan to go very far because she wasn't sure what was out there lurking in the woods. The more she thought about it, the more apprehensive she became. Maybe she should get a walking partner.

"Whatchu finna do?"

She looked in the direction of the parked vans. She made her way over to the one where Jah was sitting in.

"Why are you out here?" she asked. She eyed the blunt he was smoking.

He shrugged. He offered her the blunt.

Shaking her head, she fanned the smoke away from her. "I was about to go for a lil' walk but I'm scared. What if it's bears out there?"

"Shaky ass," he mumbled. "Ain't nothing gon' getchu."

"Well, go with me," she suggested.

He chuckled, "I ain't going out there so I can get ate the fuck up."

Jazmin laughed, "But you just said nothing was going to get me."

"I lied. Where that bald headed mufucka? Why won't he walk witchu?"

Jazmin's smile faded. "I don't wanna be bothered with him right now. Hell, he's the reason I need to take a walk."

"Y'all having a lover's fight?" Jah teased.

"No!" she said emphatically.

"Then what the nigga done did?"

"It's what he hasn't done," she said with disappointment.

A wicked grin formed on Jah's lips. "Aw, that nigga still ain't hit it, huh?"

"Shut up, Jah," Jazmin said cutting her eyes away from him.

"Here, hit this shit. It'll help; trust me," he said offering her the blunt again.

Jazmin refused again. "I can't."

"You done quit smoking?"

She nodded.

"Since when? You don't mothafuckin' drink no more either, huh? Cause last night yo' ass was drinking water and shit."

"I'm just trying to watch my weight," Jazmin lied.

"There you go with that shit," he mumbled under his breath.

"Jah shut up, okay? Nivea is skinny and you act like you're so in love with my size."

Ignoring her statement, he said, "Get in here with me."

"No," she responded.

"Get in here, Juicy," he demanded, but his voice was gentle.

Jazmin felt her body tingle when he referred to her by her nickname. Trying to read between the lines, Jazmin stared Jah back in his sultry eyes. She gave him a suspicious look, "I don't think that's a good idea."

"All I said was get in here."

"Yeah, but it's the way you said it."

Jah shrugged as if he didn't care. "Well take yo' ass on walking and get jumped by a fuckin' bear."

She groaned at herself for being so weak as she made her way around to the passenger side door. She climbed in and stared back at him. "Now what?"

"What the fuck you mean?" he asked as he put the blunt out.

"Why did you want me in here?"

"Take yo' pants and panties off," he ordered.

"No!"

"Take that shit off," he ordered once again, but more firmly.

"And then what?"

"Stop being so damn stupid."

"Jah," she spoke with frustration. She wanted to do it, but she didn't. *What if they got caught?* She opened her mouth to object but halted when she saw that Jah had moved his seat further back, the back was laid further down, and he held the thickness of his already erect dick in his hand.

"C'mon," he beckoned her.

"What about—"

"What about I'm ready to tear that pussy up. Now stop fuckin' stallin' and get on this dick!"

Damn! Jazmin thought as she felt her center aching intensely. Throwing caution to the wind,

Jazmin removed her shoes, capri leggings, and panties. With Jah's assistance, she climbed onto his lap as he worked inside her wetness. After relishing the feel of his girth, Jazmin began thrusting her hips forward to take him further inside her. It was awkward being in the small space of the front seat but she was making it work.

Jah gripped her ass as he tried to meet her every thrust. He wanted to dig in her deeper but the space wouldn't permit it. He pushed her back so that she was more upright. He told her, "Bounce on it."

She did as she was told and got so carried away she ended up leaning back and laid heavy on the horn.

Jazmin's eyes widen. She hissed, "Shit!"

"Don't you—"

Ignoring Jah's objections and tearing from his grasp, Jazmin hopped off of him and dove in the back of the van.

Jah started laughing. "Yo' ass stupid as hell!"

"Anybody coming?" she whispered.

Jah watched the front door of the chalet open and Cassie stuck her head out. He yelled, "My bad!"

A few seconds passed and Jazmin asked, "Who was that?"

"Just Cassie," he told her. He started making his way to the back. "Go all the way to the back."

Jah coaxed her on her back, in the back row bench seating. With no time to waste, he held her legs up and entered her roughly. The way her brow pinched together in a scowl, her eyes closed, and her mouth slightly opened was so damn sexy to him. But he had to remind himself, this was only a fuck. He didn't have time to get lost in loving Jazmin, but he did want to punish the pussy for having him so caught up.

Jazmin cried out as she took the abuse Jah was laying on her. She didn't want to be heard by the others but he was showing her no mercy. With his weight against the back of her legs, her feet were damn near resting on the window.

"Jah...Jah...please...," she panted.

"You want me to stop?" he asked.

"Nooo," she whimpered.

"Is this how you want that nigga to fuck you?"

She didn't respond.

"Is this how you want Sean to fuck you?"

"Nooo," she cried.

"You miss this dick, Juicy?"

She managed a nod.

"You miss me?"

Her eyes flew open. She looked up into his darkened and crazed eyes. She was afraid to answer.

"I know you don't," he panted. He raised up withdrawing from her at the same time. He ordered angrily, "Turn yo' ass the fuck over."

He was mad. She knew he was because he started handling her more aggressively and rough. She was practically hugging the side of the van and window as he pounded her relentlessly. Her cries and whimpers and even pleas fell on deaf ears. It was hurting so damn good! It was invigorating and just what she needed, but she wanted more.

Listening to the sounds he made, disappointed Jazmin because she knew once he started grunting with hard strokes he was cumming. She didn't want it to end. As a matter of fact, she wished they could go for round two inside the chalet in one of the bedrooms. But he would have to explain to Nivea and she would have to explain to Lamar.

He didn't say anything to her once he withdrew from her. He pulled his pants back up and eased back to the front of the van. Climbing back over to the front seat, he tossed her panties and leggings to her. He said to her, "Go take yo' ass walking."

It was Memorial Day and it was the actual date of Desiree's and Damien's anniversary. Everyone was enjoying themselves except Desiree. It seemed like the more people approached her with concern, the sadder she got.

Rayven finally joined the others outside by the poolside. She sat down at the bench table with Desiree. She placed a label-less prescription bottle in front of Desiree.

Desiree looked at the bottle, and then into Rayven's distressed eyes and asked, "What's this?"

"It's doxycycline. But Sean thinks he slick by ripping the label off."

"Where did you find that at?"

"It was in his stuff," Rayven answered. "And even though there's no label his dumb ass doesn't realize that pills have inscriptions on them that you can look up."

"Did you ask him about them?"

"No," Rayven mumbled angrily. She stared out at the others, including her husband having fun. He was being extra touchy with Jah's friend Nivea in the pool. Rayven looked over by the grill where Jah was talking to Damien and Rock.

"All he's gonna do is deny it," Rayven said. She let out a frustrated breath. "I'm getting tired of this trust thing with Sean. He's draining. I thought we could get close on this lil' getaway but he hasn't been intimate with me at all. Then I find these pills and I think I have the answer."

Desiree leaned in closer to whisper, "You think he got something?"

"People use doxycycline for Chlamydia. I know because I got my own bottle," Rayven said with despair.

"Oh, I'm so sorry for you, Ray," Desiree said sympathetically. "What are you gonna do?"

Tears welled up in Rayven's eyelids. She shrugged, "I don't know."

"If he's cheating on you again Ray then maybe you should considered going through with the separation."

"I don't wanna lose my husband to all these hoes and bitches that he's messing around with," Rayven said as her voice cracked.

Trying to remain understanding, Desiree said, "I totally get that. But trying to hold on to Sean may mean compromising your own happiness. Will he ever stop?"

"He will and he can," Rayven said defensively. She cocked her head to the side as she questioned Desiree. "So, you don't believe in me and Sean's marriage anymore?"

Desiree shook her head. "It's not that. Sean has been caught so many times by you and those are the situations you want me to know about. I'm sure you've been dealing with this for some time now."

"But don't judge us, Dez. You of all people," Rayven said. She grabbed the pill bottle and stood up to leave. Before walking away, she said to Desiree, "When do you plan to tell Damien that you can't have babies because you used to use abortions as a form of birth control?"

Desiree's mouth hung open with shock. Rayven's words cut her deep. When confiding in Rayven, Desiree never expected for her best friend to hurt her with it. "Really, Rayven?"

Rayven tossed her hair over her shoulders and stormed back inside the cabin.

Hurt couldn't even describe how Desiree felt. Blinking back the tears, Desiree got up and went to walk around the front of the house.

Witnessing what just occurred, Jazmin went after her sister. She caught up with Desiree as she reached the parking area. "What's wrong, Desiree? What did Ray say to you?"

Desiree wiped away her fallen tears and shook her head. "It's nothing."

"It's gotta be something. You two never fight. You'll kill me over Ray so I know something is up."

Desiree chuckled through her tears. "Don't say that, Jazz."

"It's true," Jazmin joked. "You'll snap my head off in a minute when it comes to Rayven. You didn't even want me on this trip."

"I just thought after the incident at your house that Ray would still be sensitive," Desiree explained.

143

"But you came for me too."

"I know I did," Desiree said. She averted her eyes to the ground in shame. "I was angry at the thought of you possibly being with Sean."

"But that would be between me and Ray though. And I'm not Ray's friend. I only tolerate her because of you."

"I know, but that's not what I meant," Desiree said as she took a deep breath.

Puzzled, Jazmin asked, "What are you talking about?"

"I guess...I guess...," Desiree struggled with her words as she tried to keep from crying. "I'm just angry at myself and I tried to cover my own guilt by pointing fingers."

"What guilt? What happened, Dez?" Jazmin wanted to know.

"It's Sean...And for the sake of Rayven, I try to act as though everything is cool. I put the past aside and try to forget it...But I hate him. And the thought of you being used by him sickened me too."

Even more confused but just as curious, Jazmin said, "But I saw you two together at the mall last week."

Desiree looked up in shock. "What?"

"Tanya, Cassie and I were at the mall and we saw you and Sean talking. We didn't see Rayven or Damien there with you two either."

"You saw us?" she asked in disbelief.

Jazmin nodded. "What's going on?"

"I met Sean at the mall to unleash my feelings I guess. I needed to get them out."

Jazmin shifted her weight on one leg. "You're not making sense."

"After seeing the fertility specialist and getting all these diagnostic tests done, I learned that I cannot get pregnant because I've basically shredded my uterine lining to pieces. It's so much scar tissue that an egg won't implant."

"I'm sorry to hear that," Jazmin said sympathetically. She asked, "So what does that have to do with Sean though."

Desiree looked up into Jazmin's eyes and all Jazmin could see was the shame. She said, "The scar tissue came from numerous abortions."

Jazmin gasped. "What?"

Desiree looked away as tears rushed to her eyelids again. "Yeah, the good girl isn't so innocent. I had about four abortions when I was younger. And I got one about four years ago."

"But…why?"

"They were all Sean's babies."

Jazmin was speechless. Her body tightened up as she let Desiree's admission sink in. The first emotion Jazmin felt was disbelief. The second one was hurt. But the third one was anger. She turned on her heals and went storming to the back where everyone was.

Desiree caught up with her and pulled her by the arm. Begging, Desiree said, "Please don't say anything, Jazz. Not right now! I gotta talk to Damien first. And Ray doesn't know everything. Please, not right now!"

Jazmin pulled away from Desiree trying to fight back her own angry tears. "You know what!...Nothing!...Just…Tell Damien I said happy anniversary."

Desiree watched as Jazmin stormed away in the opposite direction. Feeling somewhat relieved, Desiree wiped her face and tried to compose herself before joining the others in the back.

———————

Jazmin was so angry she couldn't enjoy the rest of that night. She hated Sean's dog ass! Not only was he screwing everything that walked, but he had fathered what would have been her nieces and nephews. All of this was just sick to her.

With her arms folded, lips tight, and leg bouncing anxiously, she tried to focus on the flat screen before her. She sat on one end of the sofa while Nivea sat at the very far end. She couldn't join in on the other's playfulness and their laughter. Every time she looked in Desiree's direction, she could see that her sister was suffering. Jazmin just wanted to scream.

Then Jah came over and made matters worse. Instead of sitting in between her and Nivea, he decided to stretch his body the length of the sofa with his head in Nivea's lap and he tried to put his feet in Jazmin's lap.

"Are you fucking serious!" Jazmin yelled as she threw his legs away from her. She jumped up from the sofa and glared at a laughing Jah. "You just think everything so fuckin' funny!"

"What climbed between yo' ass crack and bit'chu in the anus?" Jah asked while still laughing.

"I hate you!" Jazmin said and stormed upstairs.

Fuck this shit, Jah thought. With an aching and very erect dick, he quietly slipped out of the bedroom with Nivea. He went upstairs and wasn't surprised that Cassie and Rock were still up talking on the main deck. It was three in the morning. They never slept.

Going to the upper floor, all Jah had to do was step out on the upper deck that wrapped around the entire chalet. He knew which room was Jazmin's. She may have kept the bedroom door locked but the double doors that opened up to the deck were unlocked. So Jah welcomed himself into her room.

A smile spread across his face when he saw that she was sprawled out with the covers pushed down at the foot of the bed. A couple of pillows were on the floor while the others surrounded her body. Lying partially on her stomach, her body was formed into the number four. The nightshirt she had on did nothing to cover her panty covered ass. Her panties were doing a half poor job themselves because one side had rose over her ass cheek giving her a serious wedgy.

After stripping out of his clothes he contemplated if he should just fuck the shit out of her or take his time. Her juicy thighs were too irresistible not to touch. The way her legs parted gave him a nice view of her pussy print. His dick seemed to swell even more which seemed impossible. It ached and it needed to find comfort inside Jazmin.

"Juicy?" he whispered. He climbed into bed and shook her leg. "Juicy?"

"Hmm," she moaned.

"Wake up baby."

She moved just a little.

He shook her leg again but this time he let his hand slide up to her thigh. He began massaging her, enjoying the feel of her lusciousness in his hands. "Juicy, wake up."

Jazmin began moaning as the massage began to feel good to her. Jah began massaging both thighs slowly working his way up to her ass. He wasn't sure if she was fully awake but she began to poke her ass out.

"You want me to have it don'tchu, Juicy?" he teased.

Jazmin rolled over to her side and stared back at Jah. "How did you get in here?"

"Through yo' door, nigga," he told her.

Jazmin admired his tattooed body and the way his dreads hung loosely down his back. Her panties started to moisten instantly. Yes, she wanted Jah to fuck her brains out, but she didn't want to sink deeper into the lust she had for him.

"Why are you naked?"

"Cause we finna fuck," he answered.

"Where's Nivea?" she asked.

"Why you asking me 'bout the next bitch when I'm in here with you?"

"Because, you should be down there with her, fucking her," Jazmin said smartly.

"Why should I fuck her when I can fuck you?"

"You men are just so greedy and selfish," she said. Her eyes lingered on his still very erect dick as he stroked it. She chuckled, "What are you planning to do with that?"

"Can I show ya?"

"Nope. Bye Jah."

He ignored her and positioned himself over her. She looked over her shoulder and could see the playful lust in his eyes. With his bottom lip caught in between his teeth he jabbed her a few times with his erection.

Jazmin giggled. "Jah, you play too much."

"You know you want it," he whispered close to her ear.

Chills traveled through her body. "Don't do that."

"Be still," he ordered.

She tried to be still and take the kisses he placed near her ear. As always it was killing her. It didn't make matters any better when he nibbled on her lobe. "Jah!"

She found relief when he started planting kisses on her shoulder. She could feel his hardness grinding into her ass also. As a natural response she found herself grinding back.

Jazmin whimpered and groaned, "Jah, why are you doing this to me?"

He pushed her nightshirt up and started placing soft kisses on her back. He stopped long enough to ask her, "Why are you doing this to *me*?"

She flipped over on her back and looked up at him. She asked softly, "What am I doing to you exactly?"

"Same thing yo' ass have always done to me," he said. He pressed himself into her, but her panties provided a barrier.

Jazmin began removing her panties. Jah moved out of the way to assist her. He then positioned himself between her legs and hovered over her.

"I don't wanna love you," he stated bluntly.

"I don't wanna love you either," she said. She began caressing his arms and chest. She held his gaze with hers and said, "I actually hate you."

"I hate yo' juicy ass too."

Although sexually frustrated with Lamar, it didn't keep her from getting her needs fixed with Jah. Her hand traveled down his torso until she reached the hardness of his dick. She took him in her hand, stroking him gently. Her eyes shifted back to his.

Jah leaned down and kissed her once, softly on her lips. He moved back so that he could look in her eyes again. "I miss being with you and Genni."

Jazmin smiled.

"I wanna come back," he stated. He then asked, "Can I come back?"

Jazmin asked, "Are you sure that's what you want?"

"I want it mufuckin' bad, Juicy."

Still massaging and stroking him, Jazmin lifted her hips forward so that his head could graze her opening. She whispered, "I wanna feel you again."

Jah gave her what she wanted but unlike the aggressiveness in the van, he was more affectionate, passion driven, and gentle. Their lips interlocked in deep sensual kisses as his tool massaged her velvet smooth walls.

If Jazmin didn't know any better, she would have sworn they were making love. Every kiss, touch, and stroke seemed to be driven with love and passion. Even the way Jazmin would move Jah's dreads back. Everything felt so right, yet something continued to hold Jazmin back.

———

The feel of his body leaving hers roused Jazmin out of her slumber. She looked down at the foot of the bed and saw that Jah was putting his clothes back on. She felt crushed knowing that he was about to leave her just to go in the room with another woman. Jazmin was so sick of feeling that way.

"Why are you leaving?" she asked.

Jah twisted around to look at her. "Damn, I thought yo' ass was knocked out."

"I was until you moved. Are you going back to Nivea?"

"Yeah. Don'tchu think that'd be mufuckin' rude if I don't, and I invited her here?"

"I guess," she mumbled. She sighed, "I guess I should let Lamar back in here then."

"No you ain't either," Jah retorted. "Leave that nigga downstairs."

Jazmin couldn't help the smile that spread across her face. She sat up and said, "Now how fair is that?"

"I don't give a fuck about fair. I don't want no other nigga touching you. Period!"

Jazmin frowned. She wanted to tell Jah that he was right about Lamar being gay but since he wanted to have double standards she would play along. "But you get to go to your room where another woman awaits your return."

"But it ain't shit going on with me and Niv," he explained.

"I can't tell. But you know what, Jah; it don't even matter. Like I said, all of you men are selfish.

And I'm not going to continue to play sideline to none of y'all," she stated and laid back down.

"Yo' ass stupid, so shut up talking."

Jazmin sat back up to witness Jah walk out of the room without so much as another thought. She couldn't stand his nonchalant attitude sometimes. But what she did finally realize was that her feelings for Jah were deep. And now she wanted to see what they could truly have together; however, she was afraid that she had let him slip too far.

When Jah entered the room he shared with Nivea, it didn't surprise him to see that she was awake and sitting up in bed. She cut her eyes at him but he wasn't about to entertain her. He laid across the foot of the bed with his back to her.

"You should have just stayed in there," Nivea said evenly.

"Stayed in where?" he questioned without turning to face her.

"Jah, I know you were in your baby mama's room. I'm not stupid."

"Your stupidity hasn't been questioned," Jah chuckled.

"I can't stand you sometimes."

Jah grunted a laugh and closed his eyes.

"Her kicking Lamar out was a part of y'all's little game. I mean, why did you two even invite other people if this is was what you were gonna do?"

Jah finally turned to face her. "First, we ain't been playing no mothafuckin' games. Two, I don't know why she kicked that nigga out. She must've found out that mufucka a fuckin' dick in the booty ass nigga. Hell, I don't fuckin' know. Third, I wasn't tryna invite you in the first fuckin' place. You insisted on coming with me. So shut the fuck up with that bullshit you talkin'."

"But since I'm here you couldn't show me a little bit more respect?"

"And I have."

"Except for now, huh?"

"I ain't even gon' lie to yo' ass. Yeah, I was in the room with my baby mama. And yeah, I just fucked her. But Niv, don't you got a husband any mufuckin' way? I thought what we was doing was just for fun."

Nivea released a frustrated sigh. She asked, "Is it because I'm on my period? You had to go fuck something, huh?"

Jah frowned. "Okay, now your stupidity is in question."

"Fuck you, Jah," she said cutting her eyes.

"Look Niv, I'm sorry if you felt disrespected. What else do you want?"

"Nothing," she said and hopped out of bed. She went to the closet and started removing her things.

"You leaving?" Jah asked.

"Yep," she snipped. "You can do whatever you wanna do."

"Uhm...I know that. And don't think I'm 'bout to stop yo' ass either."

She stopped doing what she was doing to look at him. "I don't expect you to stop me. But can you take me back home?"

"Hell naw!" he exclaimed. "Today is my mufuckin' birthday. I ain't doing shit!"

"Oh, it is your birthday," she said snidely. "Well happy fucking birthday."

Jah remained silent as she continued to collect her belongings.

After zipping her things away securely, Nivea sat down on the bed beside Jah. She said with thought, "I know you love Jazmin. If you really want things to work with her, be serious Jah. That Lamar guy seem like a really good guy for her. Don't fuck her up and you're still on some bullshit."

"She's the *only* woman I've ever loved," Jah admitted.

"Then why are you not with her?"

"Cause she ain't never wanted me that way," he said sadly. Then he asked, "Is yo' ass still leaving?"

She shrugged.

Jah laughed, "You on some bullshit!"

"Whatever," she smiled. "I mean you're right; I do have a husband and this was for fun. And it's clear that you're crazy about Jazmin. If I stay, I'm staying with an understanding now. You go get your girl, Jah."

"So that's like you giving me yo' blessing?"

Nivea nodded.

"I wanna call yo' ass retarded but I'm not," he chuckled. "I'ma just say thank you."

———

After getting dressed for the day, Jazmin made her way downstairs. Cassie, Rock, and Tanya were in the kitchen again cooking breakfast. At the breakfast bar was Lamar. Jazmin felt bad for the way she treated him.

"Oh, look who decided to come out of their room!" Tanya teased. She looked at Lamar, "Man, what did you do to her?"

Lamar turned around to look at Jazmin. He offered her a sweet smile hoping to make amends. "Good morning, beautiful."

Jazmin sat down on the stool beside him. "You ain't gotta do all that."

"But you are beautiful and it is a good morning," he said.

"Stop, Lamar," Jazmin flatly.

He chuckled. In a lowered voice he asked, "Are you still upset with me?"

Jazmin nodded. "I am."

"Will you let me back in the room?"

She half shrugged. "I'll think about it."

Tanya leaned over the counter and asked, "Was y'all tryna make a baby this morning?"

Jazmin knew she had turned a shade of red with embarrassment. "Shut up Tanya."

Lamar looked puzzled. "She hasn't let me step one foot back in that room."

Tanya narrowed her eyes at Jazmin, "What were you doing in your room then?"

Jazmin rolled her eyes at Tanya choosing to ignore her. "Fix me a plate please, ma'am."

"Are we still going to Pigeon Forge today?" Cassie asked.

"That's still the plan," Jazmin answered. "Which reminds me; I need to go pick up the cake and take it to Alamo's."

"Does Jah know we're celebrating his birthday?" Tanya asked sneakily as she slid Jazmin's breakfast plate to her.

Lamar asked, "Oh, it's Jah's birthday? Today?"

Jazmin nodded as she eyed Sean coming in the kitchen. "Yeah, and he's such an ass I don't even wanna make him feel special."

Sean stood behind Jazmin, leaned in and whispered to her, "Can I speak to you for a minute?"

Jazmin looked at her plate, "I'm eating right now."

"It'll only take a second," Sean said.

It was something in the tone of his voice and the way he was looking at her that made Jazmin concerned. She looked at Lamar, "You don't mind, do you?"

"Go right ahead," he said.

Jazmin got up and followed Sean to the main floor arcade room. Crossing her arms over her chest, she asked, "What do you want?"

"What's up with you?" he asked angrily.

"What do you mean?"

"You've avoided me this whole time. And then you brought Lamar here but you were fucking Jah this morning," he snapped.

Jazmin was taken aback. "How do you know I was with Jah?"

"Because Lamar was down here when I went upstairs to your door. The only other person that could be making you make them kind of noises is Jah."

"Okay, so what, Sean? Aren't you here with your wife?"

"You act like we're over, Jazz."

"We are!"

"I didn't say we were. And it's pissing me off."

Jazmin blinked a few times at him to make sure she was hearing him right. "Nobody cares, Sean."

"So you don't care anymore about us, Jazz?"

She shook her head. "We're done. I don't ever wanna have anything to do with you. If I had known what you really are, I would've never given you the time and day."

"What does that mean?"

"You're the worst man a woman could ever be stuck with. And I hope Rayven leaves you."

"So does that mean you're telling her about us?"

Jazmin shook her head. "Me and you is probably the easiest thing for her to swallow."

Sean appeared confused. "What?"

"You know your dirt more than I do," she said with a raised eyebrow. "Now is that all?"

"So you don't think Genesis being in the picture won't hurt her?"

"No, not at all," Jazmin smiled. "Why would it? Genesis is Jah's child."

"What are you saying?"

"I'm saying the obvious," she said and walked away.

Chapter 9

It was late by the time they returned to the chalet. As a group they had spent the entire day out sightseeing and enjoying, and splashing around at the Dollywood waterpark.

If looks could kill, Jazmin was sure Sean had murdered her a hundred times over. He ran Lamar over probably a thousand times. He slaughtered Jah a million times. As mad as she wanted to be at Jah for having Nivea around, the fact that he couldn't keep his hands off of her made her forget why she was even mad. She thought it was odd that Nivea didn't get in the water but was totally okay with Jah being up under her.

They all migrated to the lower level billiard room. The guys were playing pool. It amazed Jazmin how they could even play being that they were drunk as hell. Even the ladies were tipsy.

"You're not drinking, Jazz?" Cassie asked. She sat down beside Jazmin at the billiard table.

"No, not right now," Jazmin said shaking her head. She looked over at Lamar in what seemed like an enjoyable conversation with Damien. He had looked over her way a few times flashing her a charming smile and giving her a wink. She was still trying to figure him and his intentions out. Something was very off about him.

Then there was Jah. He was in a good mood which was a great thing. He hinted at wanting to talk to her later but he never said what it was about. However, she did notice since being back at the rental he and Nivea were up under each other more.

And then there was Sean. Since being back he was looking crazed. It was clear that he had drank too much and it was pissing Rayven off.

Desiree cocked her head to the side and grinned suspiciously at Jazmin. "I know you're not pregnant, are you?"

Jazmin widen her eyes and looked away. "Hey, who wants to go watch a movie in the theater room?"

All of the women broke out in playful objection.

"Are you pregnant for real?" Cassie asked. She whispered, "Who the daddy?"

Jazmin dipped her chip in the spinach mixture. "I am not pregnant although Lamar and I are talking about it."

"So the two of you have made up?" Desiree asked.

"Not really. I'm still mad at him about something," Jazmin said looking over at Lamar again.

"What that nigga do?" Tanya asked.

Michelle asked, "Is he gay? I always thought he was gay."

"Why?" Cassie said giving her the side eye.

Michelle cupped her large bosom and said, "Cause he ain't never looked at these."

Everybody gave her sharp side eyes.

Tanya asked in sarcastic disbelief, "Really, bitch?"

Jazmin laughed covering her mouth so that her food wouldn't spill.

Rayven posed, "What makes you think you're God's gift to men, Michelle?"

Arrogantly, Michelle answered, "Cause I am."

Scoffing, Rayven said, "Coming from someone who's never had a man."

Michelle turned her lip at Rayven with detest. "Bitch, you always thinking your shit don't stink. I'd rather be single and fuck any mothafucking man I

169

want than to be married to a nigga that's fucking every other woman but me!"

Cassie grunted, "Umph."

Rayven rolled her eyes upward. "And here she goes with this again."

"Well, maybe if you shut the fuck up I wouldn't go there," Michelle argued.

"Ladies, let's not do this here," Desiree intervened.

Tanya narrowed her eyes towards Rayven, "Bitches like you always wanna judge somebody and ain't shit perfect 'boutcho life."

Rayven tried to smooth it over. "I'm not saying it is. I only said that because Michelle had the nerves to say that in front of Jazmin."

"I was just fucking playing any damn way," Michelle countered. "Jazmin knew that and wasn't bothered by it."

Rayven looked at Jazmin and whispered loudly so that everyone could hear, "Just watch your man."

"Bitch, you need to be watching yours!" Michelle exclaimed. She added, "That nigga going around giving everybody chlamydia and some more shit!"

Rayven's face flushed with embarrassment and shock. "What did you say?"

No one said anything. After Michelle's outburst, even the men turned their attention towards the women at the table.

Rayven turned to Desiree and snapped, "So you're going around telling my business! Why? Because I hurt your feelings about the abortions!"

"Hold up!" Desiree defended angrily. She stood up abruptly, "I didn't tell anybody anything. And thanks a lot for blurting that out!"

Damien turned towards his wife and asked, "What abortions?"

Desiree shook her head in shame, "Nothing."

"Aw shit," Cassie mumbled.

Michelle laughed maniacally, "So, Rayven got the cooties from hubby. Join the club, bitch!"

Enraged, Rayven asked, "What exactly does that mean, Michelle?"

"It means your dear ol' husband got a dirty dick and he passing shit to everybody," Michelle repeated.

"So you're fucking my husband too, Michelle? Did he pass it to you?"

Sean walked over to the table, "Ray, stop acting so ignorant. How many people are you gonna accuse of sleeping with me?"

"Get away from me, Sean!" Rayven said through clenched teeth.

"Why don't you tell her the truth," Michelle said vindictively. She gave Sean a murderous stare.

"What truth?" Sean countered. "Why don't you shut the fuck up?"

"Fuck you, Sean!" Michelle yelled. She stood to her feet causing her chair to fall over. "I'm so sick of this shit! Everybody else suffers while you get to play all innocent!"

"What is she talking about, Sean?" Rayven asked as her voice quivered.

"I don't know. Let's go to the room," Sean said. He tried pulling Rayven by her arm but she snatched it out of his grasp.

"I ain't going nowhere with you. When were you going to tell me you had chlamydia again? I had to find out when I went for my prenatal visit," Rayven sneered.

"I don't have chlamydia. What are you talking about, Ray?"

"I saw the bottle of pills, Sean! I've got my own and I ain't fucked nobody but you, my husband!" Rayven shouted.

"He gave it to me!" Michelle said angrily.

"I didn't give you shit!" Sean spat in Michelle's direction. "You probably already had that shit."

Rayven looked faint. She slowly sat back in her chair and zoned out.

"So now that's what you wanna say?" Michelle asked with a smirk.

Walking over with a pool stick still in hand, not giving the situation much thought and only concern with his own health, Jah asked Jazmin, "When the last time you fucked this nigga? 'Cause I've been fucking you raw and I know you let him hit it raw cause you wouldn't think that Genni's his. And if I got a mothafuckin' STD, I'ma beatcho ass, and I'ma beat his mothafuckin' ass too!"

Jazmin could have died. She dropped her face in the palm of her hands and sighed heavily, "Oh God!"

Everybody looked shock.

After realizing what he did, Jah's shoulders dropped with defeat and he said apologetically, "Aw shit. I'm sorry."

Desiree was livid, "You fucked my sister? Jazz, you've been fucking Sean for real?"

Jazmin looked up at her sister, "Don't Dez. You don't have a right at all."

"What does that mean, Jazz?" Damien asked.

"Talk it out with your wife," Jazmin answered.

Michelle pointed to Jazmin, "So you've been fucking Jazz and lil' Genni supposed to be your daughter?"

"Genni isn't Jah's daughter?" Cassie asked. "I'm so fucking confused right now."

Rayven burst into heavy sobbing. Jazmin felt so sorry for her but she was angrier at Sean.

"Ray, I'm sorry," Sean said but it didn't come off as sincere. They were just words. He looked over at Jazmin, "Since it's out for everybody to know, why don't you tell the truth, Jazz. Is Genesis really my baby or Jah's?"

"What!" Desiree exclaimed in disbelief.

Jazmin looked at Rayven and felt so bad. Rayven was crying uncontrollably. Nivea had come out of the media room trying to console her.

"Sean, you know who she belongs to," Jazmin answered evenly.

Sean cocked his head to the side wearing a scowl, "And I thought I knew you belonged to me too. So is she mine or is she Jah's?"

"Genni is my baby," Jah stated defiantly.

Sean looked to Jazmin for confirmation. He asked, "When did you fuck him Jazz? You talked all that loyal shit and wanting to be with me and only me but then you go fuck this nigga and make a baby that you tried to pin on me. What type of shit is that?"

"He got his mothafuckin' nerves," Tanya said under her breath.

"No, what type of shit is you sticking your dick in everybody!" Jazmin retorted.

Sean tried to rationalize the situation. "Okay, I did. I was wrong, but I'm not perfect. None of us are. I can't be condemned no more for this than any other person in this room. I fucked up because I got a problem but my love for you was real. Jah knew how I felt about you. All of the others meant nothing. But you, he knew I loved you. So for him to have fucked you behind my back is fucked up."

"Mothafucka, when it comes to Jazmin I had her first any fuckin' way. I broke that virgin pussy in," Jah shot.

Jazmin gave Jah a censorious look. *Why was he still talking?*

Sean shifted his eyes to Jazmin, "You lost your virginity to him?"

Jazmin nodded. "But it meant nothing."

Jah's mouth dropped open as he stared at Jazmin. "What?"

"We were kids," she told him.

Sean scoffed, "Why didn't you ever tell me that?"

"Because it was nothing!" Jazmin repeated in a louder voice.

Jah asked, "So when we made Genni, that was nothing too?"

"We didn't make Genni," she told him.

"You and his sorry ass sho in the fuck didn't make Genni," Jah said angrily pointing at Sean with the pool stick he held in his grasp. "Getcho ass out of the land of fuckin' denial and admit that we fucked and yo' ass got pregnant."

176

"Jah, we didn't start sleeping together until after Genni was born," Jazmin argued.

Jah shook his head in disbelief. He didn't know what hurt more; the fact that she didn't want to acknowledge that they were intimate and made Genesis, or the fact that he knew it was time to give up on her for good.

"You got that," he said angrily. Jah threw the pool stick down. "Don't fuckin' talk to me no goddamn mo'. All y'all fuckin' stupid. I don't even know why I fuck with any of y'all. Just dumb as hell but'chu wanna call me crazy!"

Jazmin felt so bad for her part in all of this. She watched Jah walk out with Nivea following. She turned back to Sean, "I hate you so much, Sean. Who haven't you fucked in this room?"

Rock raised his hand. "I ain't fuck the nigga."

"It seems like you've fucked every woman in here, Sean," Michelle said wryly.

"My shit was a long time ago," Cassie said in her defense. "I was fourteen and he didn't know what the fuck he was doing. Ain't never wanted that lil' shit again. It was before you Rayven, but I'm sorry you have to face the fact that your husband is a hoe and liar."

Tanya spoke up, "Well, I guess I'm the only one he ain't fucked besides Nivea and Sabrina. And that's fucked up. Sean, why you ain't tried to fuck me?"

Sean looked over at Tanya as if she had lost her mind. He said, "I do have some standards."

"Oh no you didn't with yo' STD leaking dick," Tanya sneered.

Sabrina pierced Sean with her gaze. "Looks like your world is crumbling."

Sean spat her way, "Oh shut the fuck up!"

Cassie said, "Wait a minute now. I know you ain't fucked the white bitch too!"

Michelle scoffed, "Sabrina been fucking Sean. Hell, she helped me fuck him a few times."

Tanya looked at Sabrina with disgust. "Bitch, I thought you was with Ricky."

Ricky spoke up, "Naw, they just didn't want you knowing she was with Sean."

"Well ain't this some shit! So yo' ass used me to come on this trip," Tanya said angrily.

Rayven stopped crying and in a trance got up from the table and walked out.

Damien looked over at Desiree, "How come you didn't deny being with Sean?"

Desiree immediately became uncomfortable. Her face turned a shade of red. "Well...I don't wanna talk about it."

"No, let's talk about it since everything else is being spilled here," Damien said folding his arms over his chest.

"Baby, it was way before you. We were younger," Desiree explained.

"So this nigga has had all of the women in this room!" Damien hollered. He was beyond pissed.

Sean's smirk didn't make anything better. Damien went after him and before anyone could intervene the two men were on the floor going at it.

While Sean and Damien were fighting, Tanya slapped Sabrina into oblivion and stormed out of the room.

Rayven returned to the billiard room. While Rock was holding Damien back and Ed and Ricky were holding Sean back, Rayven charged at Sean with a carving knife.

Cassie cried, "Oh dear God, please fix it!"

Chapter 10

With everything that transpired, it was agreed that the trip should come to an abrupt end. No one said much as they moved about. There was a lot of eye rolling and murmuring under the breath. Couples were divided, angry and in their feelings. The only people that seemed to be in a good mood were Cassie, Rock and Ricky, which was aggravating everyone.

Rayven hadn't spoken one word since she sliced Sean. She didn't seem to have any regrets either. Sean had been taken to the local emergency room and walked away with thirty-four stitches across his chest. He was in agony but no one paid him much attention. To ensure his safety on the way home, he rode in the van with Cassie, Tanya, Desiree, Ed, Ricky, and Rock. Everyone else rode silently in the other van.

Jah was still hurt by Jazmin's denial. So many times throughout the night he wanted to approach her and ask her once again. Maybe she was only playing, like she didn't remember in front of everyone else. That's what he wanted to believe. And as hurt and angry as he was, he still couldn't turn off his feelings for her that easily.

He glanced toward the front of the van where Jazmin sat beside Lamar and just looked out of the window. *Why did she make her life so complicated?* She always wanted to prove she was worthy by getting someone like Sean to notice her when the person who didn't need proof had been staring her in her face the whole time. And now look at the mess Sean created amongst everybody. Sean wasn't worth no woman's time.

It was Jah that always came to her rescue when she was being bullied when they were younger. It was Jah who told her she looked pretty even though she didn't believe him. It was him that wanted to take her to his junior prom but she turned him down. And if she hadn't dismissed him so easily, she would have known it was him who had acted as a secret admirer and left some wilted flowers and a box of candy for her on Valentine's Day when she was fourteen. She thought Desiree and her friends were playing a joke on her. She threw the flowers away and gave the candy to Tanya right in Jah's face.

And then there was the whole Genesis situation. Maybe it was easy to pretend and go along with letting Sean believe he was Genesis real father. It was Sean that she wanted anyway. At first, Jah didn't give much thought to Jazmin's pregnancy except how could she allow herself to get pregnant by Sean. It never crossed Jah's mind that he could be the father. But when he really looked at Genesis after she was first born, he knew that was his baby.

****

Downing her fourth tequila shot, Jazmin looked around the crowded room for Sean. She could have sworn he was in her view just a few minutes ago. He had been talking to some skinny girl. It angered Jazmin. Why did he extend an invite to her to attend this party when he wasn't even at her side? This party was filled with people that didn't know their situation. Who could go back and tell Rayven?

Jazmin turned back to the guy acting as the party's mixologist. "Can I get another shot?"

The guy fixed the drink and extended it out to her. When she reached for it, Jah intercepted it. As if she was moving in slow motion, Jazmin turned in his direction and yelled angrily, "That was mine!"

"Yo' ass done had enough!" Jah shouted at her.

"How you know? I just got started," she lied.

"Nigga, I've been watching you. You done drank some vodka and now you done had about five of these mufuckas. I'm finna take yo' ass home."

"I don't need you to take me home," she said cutting her eyes. "I drove my own car and I'm going with Sean."

"Where the fuck Sean at then?"

She turned to the crowd of partiers. "He somewhere out there."

"No that nigga ain't. He asked me to make sure yo' ass got home."

"He is here!" she pouted. "He told me to come. He's supposed to go home with me."

"I think he had to go back home, Juicy," Jah told her. It was a lie but he was sure that's what she would rather hear than hearing that Sean left with some random bitch.

"But why did he leave me? He didn't tell me."

"C'mon so I can take yo' ass home," he said. He tried to grab her arm but she pulled away. She ended up bumping into the person next to her.

"I'm sorry," she said meekly as she patted the person's chest. She smiled goofily up at the guy, "You gotta girlfriend?"

The guy chuckled and shook his head.

"You want one? 'Cause my so called boyfriend left me."

Jah intervened, "Man, don't mind her drunk ass."

Jazmin cut her eyes at Jah and began walking away. If the room would stop rocking she could maintain her balance. She went in the direction where she saw Sean last.

Jah watched her for a minute as she tried to push through the crowd. She didn't get very far. She bumped into another guy but this one didn't seem as nice as the first one. He had a predacious vibe about him. Jah could see he was sizing Jazmin up like she was prey. He started talking to her and whatever he said made Jazmin smile and she hugged him. He hugged her back but his hands roamed all over Jazmin's ass.

"Hol' up my nigga," Jah interrupted. "What the fuck you think you doing?"

"What's up, Jah?" the guy said. "This you?"

Jazmin answered, "No!"

"Don't mothafuckin' matter if she is or not. She ain't yours, mothafucka!" Jah spat angrily. "Take yo perverted ass on with that shit."

"Aye, I didn't mean — "

"Shut the fuck up talkin' to me," Jah said cutting his eyes. He grabbed Jazmin by her arm and pulled her through the crowd. "I'm takin' your dumb ass home."

"But Sean!"

"Fuck Sean!"

Jazmin didn't say anything else. She had to concentrate on moving her feet quick enough to keep up with Jah. He led her straight to her car and took the keys from her. He pushed her in on the passenger side and then he jumped in the driver's seat.

"I wasn't ready to leave!" she whined as Jah started driving away.

"Shut up," Jah mumbled.

"But what if Sean comes back?"

"He ain't."

"You don't know that."

"I know! Now shut the fuck up!"

"You're driving too fast and I'ma throw up!"

"Throw up. It's yo' fuckin' car. I don't care."

"I'ma throw up on you," she laughed.

"No the fuck you ain't. Throw up on me and I'ma throw yo' ass outcho own mufuckin' car."

"Do you even know where I live?"

"Juicy, I was just at yo' house with Sean the other day. Damn, you stupid when you drink!"

She giggled. "I knew that."

Fifteen minutes later they had arrived at Jazmin's suburban house.

Jah shook her. "We here."

"I can't move," she said with her eyes closed.

"Do I gotta carry yo' ass in the house?"

Jazmin opened her door and fell out.

"Goddamit!" Jah groaned.

She was laughing. "I'm good."

He walked around to her side to help her to her feet.

"I got it," she said moving away from him. As cautious as her drunk mind would let her be, Jazmin walked slowly to her porch steps. She stopped and looked back at Jah. "I don't think I can make it."

"If yo' dumb ass don't walk up them mothafuckin' steps! It's only four of 'em. Got-damn!"

She reached out for him, "Help me. I might fall."

Jah allowed her to use him as support as she ascended the porch steps. She managed to tell him which key would let them in. She stumbled in and sat on the bottom steps of her staircase. She struggled with her shoes.

"Uhm you know yo' alarm 'bout to go off, right?" Jah said. "What's the fuckin' code?"

"It's...oh fuck! I can't 'member...," she said. She grabbed the staircase railing and pulled herself up. She walked to the alarm keypad and looked at the glowing neon number pad. She keyed in zero-six-one-eight and it stopped.

"I thought you couldn't remember."

She grinned proudly, "I had to look at the numbers."

"You gon' be alright?" he asked.

"Can you call Sean?" she asked.

Without question, Jah pulled out his phone and dialed Sean. Surprisingly he answered.

"What's up?" Sean asked.

"Juicy asked me to call you," he said staring back at an eager Jazmin.

"Where she at?"

"Standing in front of me. She drunk than a mothafucka too!"

"I can't really talk to her right now."

"I already know," Jah said.

"*Just make sure she get home.*"

"*She already home.*"

"*Good looking out,*" *Sean said.* "*I gotta go though so I'll holla at ya tomorrow.*"

"*Bet,*" *Jah said ending the call.*

Jazmin frowned, "*What happened?*"

"*He couldn't talk to you man. I told you that. Now, are you straight so I can go?*"

"*He didn't wanna talk to me?*" *she pouted.*

"*He was busy. Juicy, you know how this shit goes,*" *Jah told her.*

She started crying and dropped to the floor dramatically.

Jah rolled his eyes. "*Fuck man! Getcho ass up!*"

"*No,*" *she cried.*

Jah started laughing because even though her voice sounded as if she was crying, there were no tears.

Instead of getting up and walking, Jazmin started crawling towards the back of her house.

Jah turned his head from side to side trying to capture the best angle of her ass in the black spandex skirt she had on.

"*Juicy, that ass looking real fat,*" *Jah teased.* "*I think you need to get up.*"

"*Stop looking at my butt!*" *she called.*

Jah followed her to her den that was open to her kitchen. She sat in the middle of the floor. Her skirt had rose up her thighs and he had a full view of the treasure in between them.

"Can you get up?" Jah asked as he tried to discreetly adjust himself in his pants. Her display of her goods had him on rock solid.

She stretched her arms up towards him. "Help me, Jah."

He lifted her by going under her arms. She instantly wrapped her arms around his neck. Their bodies were very close. So close that Jazmin narrowed her eyes at him and asked, "Do you got a gun?"

"No."

She reached down below and grabbed his dick through his jeans. "What's this?"

"It's my dick."

"Why is it hard?"

"Why are you still holding it?"

"Because...," she said giving it some thought. Still holding it she broke out into a smile, "It actually feel nice in my hand. But why it's in your pocket?"

Jah laughed. He pulled away from her and removed her hand. She stared down at his erection. Before he could step away from her she had grabbed it again.

"Will you stop before I have to use it," he told her.

"It seem so big!" she said as her eyes grew with wonderment. "Oh! I remember him! Do you remember, Jah?"

"I gotta go," Jah said moving her hand away again.

"No, no, no, no," she said. "Have a seat. You ain't gotta go right now. Siddown."

"Where you going?" he asked her as she walked into her kitchen.

"Siddown for a minute," she called.

Jah didn't trust himself and for sure didn't know what Jazmin was up to. He knew he needed to leave but something wouldn't let him. Maybe it was his brick hard dick keeping him in Jazmin's house.

"Juicy, what are you doing?" he asked as he made his way into the kitchen. He caught her downing another shot of her own tequila. "What the fuck are you doing?"

She laughed. "I had to have another one...Well...two more. Here, you have one."

"No, I'm good," he said.

She insisted, "Just take one. You might need it after this."

"After what?"

"Here take it," she told him.

He took it and lifted it to his lips. Jazmin went for the buckle of his belt.

"Whatchu doing?" Jah asked after swallowing down the drink.

She put her finger up to her lips and shushed him.

"Do you know what you're doing?" he asked looking down at her.

"I don't know. I just know that my pussy is hot and I need some dick. Ugh! Can you take this belt off? It ain't working."

Jah unbuckled his belt for her. "You want me to undo my jeans too?"

"Take it all off!"

"You ain't took nothing off."

"We'll get to that later."

When he pulled his dick out he waited to see what Jazmin would do. She looked up at him with big, innocent, brown eyes and smiled coyly. If he hadn't been in love with her before, he knew for a fact he was in love in that moment.

"Juicy, you sure you wanna do this?"

She nodded. Before he could ask her again, she had taken him in her mouth. Her head game was sloppy and wet just like he liked it. She didn't hold back at all. She *sucked his dick so good his voice went up a couple of octaves.*

"Goddamn, Juicy!" he whimpered. His body tensed up and he could feel his nut building. He tried to pull away but she wouldn't let up. He warned her, "I'm 'bout to cum, baby."

That didn't stop her. She sucked until he unloaded in the back of her throat. She continued to suck until he was empty. He was about ready to punch her if she hadn't let go.

Proudly, she stood to her full height and did a little bounce. "How was that?"

Angrily he asked, "Where you learn to suck dick like that?"

She placed her finger up to her lips again. "Ssh, don't tell Sean. I ain't never done that for him."

"I'm telling," Jah said playfully. He asked, "Can we go upstairs to yo room for the rest?"

She fixed herself another shot and downed it. She smiled, "Yeah."

Jah made her walk in front of him because she was stumbling again. She giggled the whole time going up the stairs. As soon as she reached her bed, she plopped down. "Whatchu wanna do now?"

"I wantchu to get naked."

Without any inhibition, Jazmin stripped down to total nakedness and waited for her next instruction. She was so cute and beautiful at the same time. Jah wanted to make her all his. And Sean would just have to deal with it.

Before he could get to Jazmin, Jah's phone began ringing. He pulled it from his back pocket to look at it. It was Sean. As he contemplated answering it, Jazmin had gotten on all fours with her ass facing him. She was teasing him and luring him in.

"Fuck that shit," Jah said rejecting the call. He powered his phone off and placed it back in his back pocket before undressing.

Jazmin's eyes were closed but she wore a smile. Her movements were sexy and enticing. It was as if she was drugged and in the land of bliss.

Jah rubbed her pussy and his dick instantly sprang back to life. She was so wet she felt like she was leaking. He bent down to kiss her cheeks then he covered her pussy with his mouth. He ran his tongue from the tip of her clit to her opening. He made sure to get in between every fold and crevice of her pussy.

It was feeling so good to Jazmin it was putting her in the most relaxing state she had ever been. With her eyes closed, she moaned loudly and quivered with every orgasmic wave that ripped through her body. When she felt his tongue tease her asshole, she gasped. She hollered out, "Aw shit now!"

"You like that?" Jah asked her.

"Yes!"

The alcohol was starting to come down on her. He was making her feel too good and she almost drifted off to sleep. If it wasn't for the feel of his dick forcing its way inside her, she would have passed out.

Her eyes flew open as he started punishing her from the back. She wasn't prepared for how he handled her. She made so much noise and was damn near in tears. She cried out, "Oh shit! This feels so good! Don't stop...don't stop!"

Jah had no intentions on stopping. He planned to take advantage of every moment of this night. But to be clear, he asked her, "Who's fucking you, Juicy?"

"You are!"

"What's my name?"

"Oh God!" she screamed.

"That's close enough."

An hour later, and after throwing up twice, Jazmin was dead to the world. Nothing he did could wake her up. He didn't want to leave her as she was or even leave her alone for that matter. After getting dressed, he *covered her up good in her bed. He laid at the foot of the bed and watched her all night until he fell asleep.*

The following afternoon when Jazmin finally decided to wake up, she found a sleeping Jah at the foot of her bed. He was fully clothed but she was naked.

She extended her leg to shake him with her foot. "Jah!"

He awakened immediately with a scowl and his eyes were red. "What nigga?"

"Can you get out so I can go to the bathroom?"

"Damn," he groaned. "I just went the fuck to sleep."

"Why were you up all night and why are you even in my bed?" she asked. She grimaced and held her head. "I think I got a hangover."

"You should. I've been watching yo' ass all night," he told her as he sat up. He looked over at her and thought she was still just as beautiful even with her hair all over her head. "You gon be alright?"

Jazmin nodded.

"You need me to do anything before I go?"

She shook her head.

"I'm finna call Ed or Ricky and see if they can come get me."

"Where's your car?"

"I drove you here in yo' car. Do you remember anything from last night, Juicy?"

"Not really," she responded. "But thank you for getting me home. I'ma cuss Sean out when I see him."

"Bet that," Jah said. He got up and walked to the bedroom door. He turned around and looked at her.

"What?" she asked.

He shook his head. "I'll holla atcha later or something."

Jah chose to wait outside for Ricky to show up. As he waited, he wondered if Jazmin remembered the night before. And if she did remember it, was she going to acknowledge it or put it aside like it never happened as she did when they were teenagers. His heart told him to talk about it with her but his gut told him to leave it alone and follow her lead. As it turned out, she chose not to remember it at all.

Chapter 11

Rock helped Sean into his house while Cassie tended to Rayven. No one thought it was wise to leave those two together for any length of time alone. The dead look in Rayven's eyes was too unpredictable. They were sure she wanted to finish what she started.

"How could he do me like this?" Rayven asked aloud as she watched Sean ascend their porch steps.

"He's a dog and don't care about nobody but himself," Cassie answered for her.

"He's not the man I married," Rayven murmured.

"Actually, he is. This is Sean. Always have been and always will be. He just had the wool pulled over your eyes all these years."

"No, he wasn't always this way. He loved me," Rayven said adamantly.

Cassie sighed, "I'm not saying that he didn't or that he don't. But Sean's first love is himself and his first needs are his own."

"Why did he marry me if he had no intentions on being the husband that I needed him to be?"

"I have a theory," Cassie said. "Do you wanna hear it?"

Rayven's eyes shifted to Cassie. "Sure."

"Sean gotta be a winner. He saw you as a prize that everybody wanted at the time. It's a competition for him. It's like a rush. Remember how all the niggas used to sweat you and you were being all picky? He was determined to get you. And when you teetered back and forward, marrying you secured the deal. After he got you, the rush died. Now I don't wanna throw this up in your face to hurt you, but Jazz got two men other than Sean in her life that wanna make her happy. Sean won't sit back and let that happen. He gotta win."

Rayven frowned. "So you're saying Sean is dead set on having Jazmin?"

Cassie nodded. She said, "He's not gonna let Jah or Lamar win her. You see how he gave no fucks about any other person's feelings last night when he was professing his love for Jazmin."

"But Jazmin?" Rayven turned up her nose. "Of all people."

"See, that's your problem Ray. That's why you can't see the shit you need to see 'cause you sit up and focus on the wrong things. There's nothing wrong with Jazmin. As a matter of fact, she's a good catch for any man. Yeah, she's struggled with her weight all her life but she looks good. Don't dismiss her because she ain't a size six like your skinny ass."

"Size four," Rayven corrected.

Cassie turned her lips up at Rayven and looked down at the swell of Rayven's belly. "You a size four still with all that belly?"

"I can still wear some of my pants."

"Girl, don't suffocate that baby in them little pants," Cassie joked.

Rayven fell quiet as she gave Cassie's words some thought. She asked, "Do you think Genni is Sean's baby?"

"Hell no!" Cassie said. "Jazmin play too much. She know Genni is Jah's baby."

"How could she be with two friends though? That's just so wrong."

"Ask Sean how could he sleep with his wife's friends," Cassie countered. She said, "I'm not saying no one person was right in any of this. Everybody was wrong. That's the one thing I will agree with

Sean on. But don't concentrate so much on everyone else's faults without questioning Sean's. Ultimately, he's the one that's obligated to honor, respect, and love you. Jazmin don't owe you shit. Y'all not even really friends."

"But she smiled in my face and talked to me knowing that she was screwing my husband."

"And your husband came home to you every night smiling and telling you he loved you, knowing he had just screwed another woman. You wanna be mad, be mad at that nigga that you stabbed like a boss," Cassie said. She started giggling at her own statement.

Rayven cut her eyes at Cassie, "That's not funny."

"It wasn't last night, but it is now," Cassie laughed.

Rayven headed toward the porch.

"Where you going?"

"In here to talk to my husband," Rayven called over her shoulder.

Cassie followed her into the house. They found Rock and Sean sitting in the den. Sean was being so dramatic as if he was in ICU. Cassie rolled her eyes and took a seat beside Rock on the sofa.

Rayven sat down in the reclining chair. She looked at Rock and Cassie and said, "Can I speak to my husband in privacy?"

Sean objected, "Noooo!"

"Yeah, that might not be a good idea," Rock said.

Rayven said, "Fine. Sean, I didn't mean to cut you as bad. I was angry and hurt and in a state of shock. Like, how could you do this to me?"

"I don't know, Ray," Sean mumbled. "I have no answers for you right now."

"We have a baby on the way," Rayven stated.

"I know."

"Do you think Genni is really yours?"

Sean shrugged. "There's a possibility. Don't know."

"So what was going to become of our marriage?"

"I don't know, Rayven. You can divorce me if you want to."

"Is that what you want? Were you planning to divorce me for Jazmin?"

Sean shrugged again.

Rayven lowered her eyes and focused on her hands. "Do you love Jazmin?"

"Ray," Sean groaned.

"When did you stop loving me, Sean?" Rayven demanded to know.

Cassie didn't like how calm Rayven was acting. She kept her eyes on Rayven in case she would have to intervene.

"I love you, Rayven," Sean said. "And I'm going to love our child. But I don't know if I'm right for you."

"When did this occur to you? Before or after all your dirt was brought to the forefront?"

"Both, I guess."

"What does that even mean, Sean?"

"It means I've always thought it. I knew what I was doing wasn't right or fair to you but I wasn't ready to just let go."

"Cake and eat it too, huh?"

"Something like that."

"So what now, Sean?"

He shrugged.

"You're not going to leave your little women alone, are you?" Rayven asked. "Or are you in love with Jazmin now?"

Sean avoided Rayven's gaze. His first impulse was to lie but the idea of losing Jazmin completely to Jah or Lamar was just too overwhelming to dismiss.

Before anybody could prevent it, Rayven grabbed a small picture frame of her and Sean from the end table and slung it towards Sean. It hit him right in his bandages.

"Oh shit! She gon kill 'im!" Cassie exclaimed as she jumped up. She grabbed Rayven before she could charge at Sean.

"Get out!" Rayven cried. "Just get out and don't ever come back! I hate you, Sean! You've made a fool out of me for the last time!"

In spite of his pain, Sean jumped up from the sofa and headed for the door. "I'll gladly leave because I'm not staying here with you!"

Rock pointed to his chest, "You're bleeding. I think she busted your stitches man."

Rayven reached for the lamp but Cassie took it from her. "I'm going to do more than that before it's over with, you dirty bastard!"

Cassie urged, "Just get him out of here!"

After dropping Tanya off, Jazmin had to go get Genesis. She missed her baby so much.

"So how was she?" Jazmin asked as she adored her daughter in her arms.

"She was perfect," Phyllis said. "She was no problem at all."

Jazmin placed a kiss on Genesis' head. "Mommy missed you so much!"

"So how was the trip?" Phyllis asked. "And why are you back so early?"

Lamar said with a raised eyebrow, "The trip was very eventful."

Phyllis looked between Lamar and Jazmin. "What happened?"

"It was good until last night," Jazmin explained.

"Did Jah say something about the two of you?" Phyllis asked.

"Well, you know Jah wasn't happy about that but he had someone there with him anyway," Jazmin said. "But some other things transpired. I don't even know where to begin."

"Rayven sliced her husband with a knife," Lamar blurted out.

Phyllis gasped with alarm. "Are you serious? What for?"

Jazmin shot Lamar a look. She wasn't really prepared to tell Phyllis everything. "Can I talk to you about it another time? Right now, I just wanna get to my own house and relax and catch up with my baby."

"Sure," Phyllis said. She smiled at Lamar, "Well, I'm glad she has you around."

"Yeah," he said with a smile.

Jazmin rolled her eyes. She was still mad at him too but she was glad he was there.

On the drive to Lamar's place, he asked, "So are you ready to talk about what went down last night?"

"Not really," Jazmin mumbled.

"I guess I'm a little confused about some pieces to the story. So you were sleeping with Sean. And he was one of the guys you said was fighting over the paternity of Genesis?"

"Yes. Sean's Genesis father but Jah stepped up and claimed her."

"But why does Jah thinks he actually fathered her?"

Jazmin shrugged.

"Did you sleep with him?"

"Yes, I have slept with him," she answered.

"No, I'm talking about did you sleep with him around Genesis' conception?"

Jazmin was growing irritated. She could have sworn she told him she didn't really feel like talking about any of it. "Maybe I did...I don't know...I don't remember."

"How is that, Jazz?"

"It might have been a time when I had a little too much to drink and..."

"And Jah took advantage of you?"

That sounded good but she knew it wasn't exactly the truth. She nodded in agreement and said, "That could be the only explanation about why he's so adamant that Genesis could be his, however, I wouldn't label it as Jah taking advantage of me."

"I'm not sure of how I should feel about that," Lamar said with thought.

"What do you mean?"

"I mean if you were incapacitated at the time, then that's basically rape, Jazmin. I'm not too fond of Jah as it is. I don't think he's the appropriate father figure for Genesis anyway. If I had to deal with someone I'd rather it be Sean."

"But you're not dealing with either one; I am," Jazmin pointed out.

"But if you and I pursue a serious, exclusive relationship, then I would have to deal with Genesis' father in some way."

"And I get that, Lamar," Jazmin said. She pulled up to his apartment building and put her car in park. "But since Genesis has been born, Jah stepped up in a major way and has taken care of her. I mean, he fixed bottles, changed diapers, washed her clothes, and stayed up feeding her. Despite what has happened between him and me, I can't deny that he loves Genesis."

"Why don't you get a DNA test, and if he's indeed Genesis' father, then let the courts mediate between you two as parents," Lamar suggested.

Jazmin asked, "You don't want me to have any dealings with Jah anymore?"

"If it isn't' necessary then why bother with him? The man has a few screws loose, Jazz. You know that. He's too volatile. I mean...unless you have those kind of feelings for him."

Jazmin gave it some thought. She did love Jah; more than she was willing to admit. And then there was the fact that she was carrying his child. But she knew she hurt him too many times. He probably wouldn't give her another opportunity.

"Lamar, I respect Jah in spite of his crazy ways. He's a good guy; just don't fuck with him."

"So does that answer mean you don't have romantic feelings for him?"

At this point, she didn't feel like she owed Lamar any explanations about her feelings. He hadn't even bothered to have sex with her. Jazmin wasn't sure what Lamar intentions were.

"Jazz, I know you've been upset with me because we didn't have sex but there's a reason for that," Lamar said.

He must've been reading my mind, she thought.

"I wanted to tell you but I couldn't bring myself to say it out loud. It's rather new to me and I haven't gotten used to it myself," he said with uneasiness.

Jazmin became concerned and turned to face Lamar. "What is it? Are you dying?"

He chuckled lightly, "No, not yet anyway."

"Then what is it?"

"I have MS and in my case I also suffer from ED," he stated. "It was why I pulled away a couple of years ago in the first place."

"ED?" Jazmin scrunched up her nose.

Lamar released a defeated breath. "Erectile dysfunction."

Jazmin covered her mouth and gasped. "Oh! Lamar, I'm so sorry. Why did you let me be so mean to you?"

"Well, I wasn't ready to explain it to you anyway," he told her.

"I feel so bad now," she said. "I mean…I'm so sorry but…There's nothing…Geesh!"

Lamar offered her a smile, amused by her awkward cuteness. "Don't consume yourself with that. But I thought I should let you know so you'll understand. And at this point it's up to you if you still want to pursue something deeper with me. And yes, I would still love to be with you and have that family together."

Genesis started fussing from the backseat.

Jazmin looked at Lamar, "I guess there's a lot for me to consider."

"It is, and I want you to really think things through," he said to her. "Because once we begin this journey together, there'll be no turning back."

———

When Jazmin arrived at her house, she was surprised to see Sean's red Challenger sitting in her driveway. She grew annoyed just from the sight of the car. Ignoring his presence, she let herself into her garage. He must have moved quickly because before she could push the button to close the garage he had already ducked inside. He stood outside her passenger side door waiting for her to step out.

If it wasn't for Genesis fussing in the back seat Jazmin would have left him standing outside her car.

Getting out, she asked, "Why are you here?"

"I don't have anywhere else to really go," he said.

For a split second she felt sorry for him. He looked so sad. And the pain from his wound had him looking like he needed to take a shit. She chuckled at that observation.

"So you decided that coming here would be okay?" she asked with sarcasm. She retrieved Genesis and her belongings from the car. She would come to get her things later.

"How's babygirl doing?" he asked.

"She's doing okay. She's hungry and sleepy," Jazmin said as she let herself into her house.

When Sean followed right in behind her she looked at him, "I don't recall inviting you in."

"C'mon, Jazz," he said desperately walking around her. "I know you hate me right now but I wouldn't be here if I didn't seriously have somewhere else to go."

With Genesis still in one hand, Jazmin went to her alarm system's keypad to key in the code. She turned back to Sean. "What happened? Rayven put you out?"

"She told me to get out but I also needed to leave. I just left the emergency room because she busted my stitches," he said. "Staying around her is not safe for me right now."

Jazmin burst into laughter as she placed Genesis on the dinette table. "I mean, you say that like somebody should be sympathetic. She need to kill you."

Sean cut his eyes, "Jazz, it's not funny. She could have really killed me last night."

"What did you tell the emergency room people this time?" Jazmin wondered.

"I just made up something," he said with annoyance. Sitting at the dinette table, Sean turned Genesis' carseat carrier around so that he could look at her. She immediately saw him come into view and started fussing and cooing.

"She's definitely Jah's baby. I see it now," he said.

Jazmin responded, "All that matters to me is that she's my baby. Besides, when there was no question of her paternity, you weren't here as her father anyway."

"I was going to be," Sean answered. He looked back at Genesis, "I wish she was mine."

"Why? Because it's okay to be her father now since everybody knows about us?"

"Look, if you and I can still make this work, she's still going to be like a daughter to me," Sean said.

"You and I make this work?" Jazmin asked. She started moving about in the kitchen to get Genesis a bottle together. "You think I want something with you now?"

"It's what we always wanted, Jazz. This is the right time to go ahead and pursue this."

Jazmin shook her head. "I don't get you Sean. Shit, I don't even get me. Like, why in the hell are you even in my house and I'm talking to you like it's cool."

"Because, you know as well I know that you have love for me. Hell, you're probably still in love with me even though Jah tried to get you to fall in love with him."

Jazmin grunted a disbelieving laugh. "Are you serious? Once I found out about you and Desiree, I became done with you."

"Me and Desiree?"

"Don't act stupid, Sean," Jazmin said. Her phone rung and she quickly glanced at it lying on the kitchen counter. It was Jah but she wasn't ready to speak to him. She hit reject. She looked at Sean and continued, "Desiree told me in so many words that you two messed around back in the day and she aborted a few of your babies. And if I know you like I think I know you, I'm sure you're the one that encouraged her to get the abortions. You are so low down, Sean. How do you live with yourself?"

"I agree with you. And I live with myself by not giving a fuck. I was taught early on how not to give a fuck," he said solemnly. "I've done some rotten things to people; even my own mama and daddy, but it's what they taught me and my brothers. And because of that, one brother is dead and the other one is doing life in prison. I don't want to end up like neither one of them. I need somebody that's going to help me, Jazz."

She looked at him and felt the sympathy she wanted not to feel. "You'll be okay, Sean. But if you wanna change, it's something you have to realize from within. It's too late for us, but it's not too late for you to get your act together for the next woman. Who knows, maybe you and Rayven can make amends and heal together. She's about to have your baby in a few months. You need to prepare for that."

Sean looked at her with tear rimmed eyes and asked, "So, we're over?"

Jazmin hated herself for being such a softy. First Lamar and now Sean's scumball ass. "Sean...," was all she could say. Her phone filled in the empty silence. Once again it was Jah. She quickly hit reject. "I tell you what," she said. "I'll allow you to stay here for a few days so you can figure out where you need to go from here."

"I love you, Jazz," Sean said.

Reaching for Genesis, Jazmin said, "I love you too, Sean. It's gonna be alright. I promise."

Why wasn't she answering the phone? It was frustrating Jah. All he wanted was to be able to see Genesis. He missed his baby and he hadn't laid eyes on her in over a week. He told himself that he didn't want to go without seeing his child for long periods of time like his father had did him and Sheena. That's not the type of father Jah wanted to be.

"She still isn't answering?" Nivea asked.

They were sitting in his car outside his aunt's house. He had just arrived. Strangely the house looked very dark and without life inside. Only Uncle Leon's truck was parked in the driveway. He brushed any alarming notions aside and focused back on the other matter on his mind.

"Nope," Jah said. "All I wanna do is see my baby man."

"Are you sure that's all?"

"For now."

"So Jazmin denies that you two were together?"

"That's what her ass tryna do but I know better. She know we fucked; she just wanna be in denial for Sean's mothafuckin' ass."

"But what if she doesn't remember for real, Jah?"

"She remember. I ain't tryna hear that bullshit," he said. He could feel himself growing agitated with the situation all over again. "She bet not try to keep Genni from me either."

"Well, just keep trying. She'll answer sooner or later," Nivea said. She went for the door handle. "I guess I need to take my tale on in the house. For what it's worth, I had a good time up until last night of course."

"Bet," Jah mumbled. He looked down at his phone as he dialed Jazmin's number again.

"Try to have a good night," Nivea said before exiting the passenger door. She retrieved her things from the backseat and headed to her house.

To Jah's surprise, Jazmin's phone answered. Not giving her time to say anything, he started snapping. "Nigga, you see me mothafuckin' callin' yo' ass! Why the fuck you ain't been answering?"

"She's busy right now."

Jah fell silent and thought to himself, *I know this bitch ass nigga ain't at Jazmin's house!*

"I can take a message for you though," Sean said, smugness oozing from his voice.

"What the fuck you doing over there?" Jah asked angrily.

"Me and Jazz making up and I came to see Genesis."

"Get away from my mothafuckin' daughter ol' bitchassnigga. I'm on my way over there and when I see you I'ma beatcho ass!"

Sean started laughing. "Uhm the jury's still out on her paternity, Jah. Genesis can still be my daughter."

"How nigga? She don't even look like yo' ugly ass."

"I see it a little."

"Fuck you. Put Jazmin on the phone."

"I told you, she's busy. I'll let her know you called but I doubt she's ready to talk to you. She and I got some real making up to do, if you know what I mean."

Jah was about to respond but he heard Jazmin's voice in the background.

"Sean, are you hungry? I'm kinda sorta starving…And you should be lying down—"

"I know Jazz," Sean interrupted.

There was some rustling and their voices muffled so Jah couldn't hear anything for a few seconds.

Sean came back on and said, "Well, I gotta go 'cause my woman wants to take care of me."

Oh, both of them had Jah fucked up! Jah ignited his car back to life and was about to back up until his aunt's car pulled in behind him. She got out of the car and walked to his door.

"When did you get back?" she asked. She seemed out of breath and a little frazzled.

"Just now, but I'm bout to go to Jazmin's house and beat her and Sean's ass," Jah told her. He frowned and asked, "What's wrong with you? Where you coming from?"

"Oh...I was...Have you been inside yet?" she asked with uneasiness.

"Naw. Who in there? Hell, I thought nobody was in there for a minute."

Georgia let her shoulders drop with defeat. Sadly she said, "Jah, look. There's something I need to tell you before you go in there."

"What?"

She looked at Jah and tried to let her eyes answer for her.

"Is it Sheena?" Jah asked as the answer sunk in.

"Jah, she didn't want to ruin your trip or your birthday so she asked me not to call you and—"

"Is she gone?" he asked frantically, his voice cracking.

Georgia shook her head, "Not yet."

Chapter 12

The first thing Jazmin did every morning upon awakening was grab her phone and scroll through it. She had to make sure she hadn't overlooked any missed calls or texts. Three days had passed since returning from the disastrous trip and she hadn't heard from Jah at all. It was now Sunday.

At first she called herself giving him his space, although she had come off like she was mad with him. She couldn't really be mad at him. Everything was bound to come out eventually. She just hated that he blurted her involvement with Sean out the way that he did. And then there was him being adamant about them sleeping together to produce Genesis. That was still bothering her. She needed to talk to him about the whole situation. Besides, she was missing him like crazy.

Jazmin decided to send him a text: **we need to talk**

She got out of bed and walked across the hall to Genesis' room. Genesis was wide awake concentrating on the mobile above her.

Jazmin smiled, "How come you didn't cry for Mommy?"

Genesis turned her head to look at Jazmin and gave her a half smile, half frown. Jazmin's heart melted as she realized it was time to accept that Genesis was indeed Jah's child.

"I've been so stupid, Genni. Your daddy probably hates me right now. And you've been trying to tell me all this time. I should have listened. How are we gonna get your daddy back?"

"What does that mean?"

Jazmin whipped around to see Sean, shirtless, standing in the doorway.

She rolled her eyes and groaned, "You're still here."

"Don't do that, Jazz. You know I haven't left yet."

"Have you reached out to Rayven to see where her head is at, Sean? Cause you know I only said a few days but it's going on a week."

"I know but I don't think it's safe for me to go home yet. I've reached out to Rayven. We've talked a little. I'm supposed to go to her doctor's appointment with her next week."

Jazmin smiled as she lifted Genesis from her crib. "That's good to know. That's some progress."

"But I don't want her," Sean stated definitely.

"And that may be what's best," Jazmin said as she brushed past him. She went back into her room and placed Genesis on her bed. Genesis immediately started suckling on her fist and cooing.

Sean followed Jazmin into her bathroom. "I want you and I wanna work things out with you."

"Sean," Jazmin sighed. She proceeded to brush her teeth and look at his reflection through her vanity mirror.

"Jazz, I still love you. I'm in love with you. I can't just let you go."

She continued to brush her teeth. Her phone rang and she hurried to retrieve it from her nightstand. Muffled with a mouthful of sudsy toothpaste, she answered, "Hello?"

"Well hello beautiful?" Lamar sang into the phone.

"Hey!"

"Did I catch you at a bad time? Why do you sound like that?"

Jazmin went back to the bathroom to spit. She said into the phone, "I was brushing my teeth."

"Oh. So are we still on for today?"

"Yeah," she said.

Sean asked, "Who is that?"

Lamar asked, "Who was that?"

Geez, Jazmin thought. She said to Lamar, "Let me finish getting myself together and I'll call you right back."

"Uhm…sure," Lamar said with uncertainty.

Jazmin ended the call and looked over at Sean. "Why are you so nosey?"

"Cause I need to know who's calling my woman," he stated.

"Are you serious?" Jazmin laughed. "I'm not your woman."

"Come on, Jazz. Stop playing," Sean said.

"I'm not," she said. She washed her face off as Genesis started becoming more demanding.

"So I guess you're going to make up with Jah?" Sean inquired.

Jazmin went back into her room and picked Genesis up. "Ooh, you need a changing lil' girl."

Sean sat on Jazmin's bed and watched her go back and forth, tending to Genesis. He eyed Jazmin's body in her little blue boy cut pajama shorts. His dick needed some attention and he hadn't felt the inside of Jazmin in two months.

Sean said, "Jazmin, you're looking good bae. How much weight have you lost?"

After changing Genesis she picked her up and frowned in thought. "I'm not sure. But it doesn't matter because I'm about to pick it all up again."

"Not if you continue to do whatever it is you've been doing," he said.

Jazmin chuckled as she headed out of the bedroom. "I'm pregnant, Sean."

"What?" he asked as he followed her downstairs.

"I'm pregnant," she repeated as she headed into the den. She placed Genesis in her bouncer and headed to the kitchen.

"Are you keeping it?" he asked.

She looked up at him. "Why would you ask me that?"

"Cause it's by Jah," he answered.

She chuckled with a shake of the head. "Genesis is Jah's child too. So what?"

"So you're admitting that he's Genesis' father now?"

She continued to make Genesis a bottle. "It's obvious that he's her father. I won't keep denying it. It's not fair to Genni and it isn't fair to Jah."

"Fair? What about fair to me? So you betrayed me and fucked Jah behind my back!"

Jazmin didn't like Sean's hostility but she wasn't going to let him see her fazed. She went over to Genesis and cradled her so she could feed her. "Sean, I don't remember every single detail but I'm certain Jah and I slept together the night of Ricky's party last year. Remember you left me. All I know is the following morning I woke up with a hangover and Jah was there."

"And what makes you so sure you fucked him?"

"I was naked and I still had a sore and wet vagina. Does that answer your question?" she stated without remorse or hesitance.

Sean's enragement was written all over his face. "So you fucked Jah."

"I think that's what I said," she said smugly.

"If you knew this than why did you deny it for so long, Jazz? Why did you want me to believe I was Genesis' father?"

"Because I thought I needed you in my life!" she shouted startling Genesis in the process. Jazmin lowered her voice. "I wanted her to be yours so bad! Did it cross my mind that Jah could be Genesis' daddy? Yes, it did, but I pushed that shit way in the back of my head. I hated the idea of Genesis being Jah's. I wanted you! So I refused to see it. I maintained my innocence and I didn't wanna see it. It was wrong and I owe Jah a big ass apology. I love him too, Sean. He's been everything for me; more than you've ever been. And I never acknowledged him in my life even before all of this. So in many ways, I'm just as bad as you. I'm scum and I understand if Jah never wants to talk to me ever again."

Sean remained quiet as he let all of what she said sink in.

There was silence except for Genesis' sucking on her bottle.

The doorbell rang.

Still holding Genesis, Jazmin got up and went to the front door. She answered it.

"Why is he here?" Desiree asked pointing to Sean's car in the driveway.

"Hell, I don't know. Will you make him leave for me?" Jazmin chuckled.

"You shouldn't have let him in your house. I thought you said it was only for a couple of days," Desiree said stepping inside.

"Well…your friend still wants to kill him I think," Jazmin said turning to head back into the den.

"Uhm…she and I are over with as of last night," Desiree said following behind her.

"Really?" Jazmin said with amusement.

Desiree stopped at the den's entrance. She turned her nose up at Sean. "You're not dead yet?"

"Are you able to get pregnant yet?" Sean shot back.

Jazmin's and Desiree's mouths dropped open.

"Oh, that was low down!" Jazmin shouted.

"Fuck you, Sean!" Desiree screamed. She went after him but he ran into the kitchen and stood on the other side of the kitchen table.

Sean spat angrily, "I'm not gonna let y'all keep taking shots at me when you're just as guilty."

"But that was cold, Sean," Jazmin stated. Looking at him with disappointment, "It's time for you to leave."

"And go where, Jazz?" Sean asked hopelessly.

"I don't know. Go see if Ricky or Rock got some space for you to crash at their place," Jazmin suggested.

"Okay," Sean said with thought. He looked at an angered Desiree and said, "I'm sorry and that was below the belt. Can I just get past you without no problems?"

"Let him go," Jazmin said to her sister.

Sean eased around the table cautiously. He looked over at Jazmin and asked, "Before I go, can I ask if you're so sorry about Jah, where does Lamar fit in all of this?"

"That's none of your business, sir," Jazmin answered.

"Okay, Jazz," he said cutting his eyes. "Remember, I love you and I'm willing to let go of everybody and everything else for you. When Jah fucks up, you're gonna come looking for me."

Desiree scoffed. "I won't let her. Goodbye, Sean."

Jazmin studied her reflection in her bedroom mirror. She was looking rather slim these days but it would be no time before her stomach started swelling with life again.

She thought she looked nice for a simple Sunday brunch date with Lamar. He had asked her out because he said there was something he really wanted to talk to her about in person. She agreed only because she really felt bad about his medical situation; however, she decided that she would go ahead and tell him about her feelings for Jah as well.

Descending the back staircase into the den, she asked Desiree, "How do I look?"

"You look good, Jazz," Desiree said with a smile. She narrowed her eyes at Jazmin playfully. "Are you sure you're not trying to win this man over?"

"I'm positive," Jazmin said.

"Well, the way that dress is hugging you says differently," Desiree teased.

"I can't help I was blessed with Mama's hips and ass," Jazmin joked.

Desiree laughed, "You got that right. I guess I took after the Foster and Delgado women."

"No, I think you were just adopted cause Aunt Mary and Aunt Sarah got bodies," Jazmin laughed.

"Oh shut up!"

Jazmin smiled lovingly at her sister. Something between them had changed. Jazmin actually felt connected to Desiree for the first time. It was unfortunate that it came about due to the circumstances, but Jazmin was accepting of it.

"So, how is Damien today?" Jazmin asked.

"He's still isn't really speaking to me," Desiree said with sadness.

"He'll come around," Jazmin assured her.

"Well at least he hasn't packed up and left. I guess that's a positive."

"He's not going anywhere. He loves you too much and that man lives to make you happy. I mean, if I was him I woulda left your bossy tale a long time ago."

Desiree laughed lightly. "I am not bossy."

"Says who?"

"Okay, maybe a little."

Jazmin bucked her eyes, "Maybe a lot. Ask Daddy."

Desiree's smile faded and she wore an uneasy look. "Jazz, I just wanna say I'm sorry for being so mean to you all these years. And no matter how mean I was you were still always there for me, trying to be lil' sis."

"Oh, don't worry about it. Let's just focus on this point forward. We can make up for lost sister time. It'll be fun."

Desiree offered a small smile. "I still want a baby. I hope Damien still wants it. We may need a surrogate if in vitro doesn't work."

"Ask Tanya. She'll carry a baby for you," Jazmin laughed.

"Hell no!" Desiree exclaimed. "She smokes and has bad eating habits."

Jazmin shrugged, "I tried to help you."

Desiree asked, "What about you? Would you do it for me if it came down to it?"

"I can't right now," Jazmin chuckled.

"Why not?"

"Because I'm pregnant already."

Desiree gasped. "Get out! So you and Lamar are serious?"

"No! I haven't even had sex with Lamar. When I went for my six week checkup Dr. Bradshaw told me I was pregnant."

Desiree frowned, "Is it Sean's?"

Jazmin shook her head. "I hadn't slept with him either. It's Jah's."

"Oh," was all Desiree said.

"And Jah doesn't know but I need to tell him."

"Yeah, you do. I'm sure Jah would be happy. And Jazz, I know I've had a bunch of mean things to say about Jah, but what I said in the store that day remains the same. Jah really loves you. And even though Nivea was with him this past week, he wasn't really into that girl. He kept his eyes on you the whole time."

"How do you know?"

"Me and Damien watched him," Desiree laughed. "And by the way, we saw you two getting busy in the van also."

Jazmin gasped with embarrassment. "What did you see?"

"We only saw when y'all were in the front seat until your big booty honked the horn."

232

"Oh my God!" Jazmin chuckled shaking her head.

"It's okay. It inspired me and Damien to get our freak on," Desiree grinned.

"Let me get out of here," Jazmin said. "Are you sure you're going to be okay taking care of Genni."

"Yes. Her Tee-tee got her," Desiree insisted.

"Okay, and thanks Dez," Jazmin said sweetly.

"No problem. Enjoy yourself."

———

Before meeting Lamar at The Garden Brunch Café on Jefferson, Jazmin had to make a quick stop elsewhere. Although she was interested in what Lamar wanted to talk about, her mind continued to drift to Jah. He hadn't responded to her texts and still wasn't answering her phone calls.

Jazmin walked into the condominium building's reception area and discovered there was no attendant on duty. Since she already knew Jah's unit, she took the elevator to his floor. She felt a little nervous but she knew she needed to see him.

Standing before his door, she gathered herself and let out a deep breath. She knocked and waited. She knocked again.

Feeling disappointed, she turned to walk away just as the door opened. A female, the same female from the first time Jazmin came by peeked her head out.

Wearing a smile she said, "Was that you?"

"Uh...yeah," Jazmin said. "I was looking for Jah."

"Oh...well he's not here. Can I give him a message for you?"

Jazmin started to tell her no but she said, "Could you tell him Jazmin came by looking for him?"

The lady smiled and said, "Sure. I love your shoes by the way."

"Thanks," Jazmin said as she turned to walk away.

A part of her wanted to cry but another part of her wanted to kick her own ass. With the lady living with him, Jazmin was sure he had moved on. It may have been over for them as a couple but she wouldn't stop trying to reach out to him as a friend and figure out how they were going to do this parenting thing.

After seeing the lady at Jah's place, Jazmin started looking forward to seeing Lamar. At first she was so sure she was going to tell Lamar about her pregnancy but she decided to withhold that information a little longer.

When she walked in the restaurant and approached the table, he stood to greet her like the perfect gentleman.

"You look lovely," Lamar beamed.

She smiled as she took her seat, "Thank you. So what is it that you have to talk to me about?"

Lamar took his seat. "Well, you don't waste any time, huh?"

She laughed. "I'm just curious about what you have to talk about."

"How about we order and eat a lil' something first?" he suggested.

"I guess so," she feigned disappointment and pouted.

Lamar looked her over with a glimmer in his eyes. "You are looking really good, Jazz. I like your hair like that too. It's becoming on you."

Jazmin scrunched up her nose. Her hair was pulled atop her head in a messy but flirty bun with tendrils of hair falling here and there. "This? Jah says it looks like a bird's nest."

Lamar rolled his eyes. "Let's not bring him up, please. I want to enjoy my time with you."

"Okay," she said meekly.

The waiter came over and took their orders. After he left, Lamar said, "Are you sure you should be eating French toast and pancakes?"

"The banana foster pancakes are my favorite!" she crooned. "And I just gotta have the French toast. For some reason I want a lot of carbs lately."

"That's not good. You have to watch those carbs, baby," Lamar said.

"Lamar," she said flatly. "Don't chastise me about my food choices, please."

He threw his hands up in surrender. "I'm just looking out for you. You're the one that will complain about the weight gain. And you look amazing now. You don't want to ruin your hard work."

"I won't overindulge. I doubt I'll eat it all anyway," she said with a dismissive shrug.

Lamar reached in the front pocket of his slacks and withdrew a small black velvet box.

Jazmin's eyes shifted to the box and then to his eyes. "What's that?"

Smiling, Lamar said, "Look, I know I said let's eat first but I want to go ahead and get this out of the way. I've been thinking a lot about us lately. I love you, you know that. I've always loved you. We were good together. I wasn't ready then, but I'm ready now. And this time I don't want to lose the opportunity to make you all mine. So with that being said, Jazmin, will you marry me?"

Jazmin let her mouth drop open as he revealed the brilliant cut diamond solitaire ring. She didn't know how many carats it was but it looked really expensive.

"Lamar, are you serious?" she asked.

He was grinning. He removed the ring and placed it on her left ring finger. "I'm very serious. So what do you say?"

Jazmin held her hand out and admired the way the ring looked on her finger. "I don't know what to say?"

"Just say yes," he told her.

"I don't know what to say," she repeated.

"I figure we should make it all official before we begin making babies. And by the way, I want us to go ahead in look into some options for that."

Jazmin started fidgeting with the ring on her finger nervously. "Uhm... about that...there's some — "

Her phone started ringing. She held her finger up signaling for him to give her a second. "Can you hang on? Hello?"

"Jazz!"

It was Tanya. She sounded frantic.

"What is it?"

"Have you talked to Jah at all?"

"No, I haven't heard from him."

"Well you need to. He's fucked up, Jazz. Where are you? Can you meet me?"

"Wait! What do you mean I need to and he's fucked up? What's going on?"

"It's Sheena. She's about to die any day now. He need you Jazz."

Jazmin's heart dropped. "Where is he?"

"They're at his aunt Georgia's," Tanya said. "I'll meet you there."

"Okay," she said and ended the call. Without explaining to Lamar she grabbed her purse and got up.

"Hey! What's going on?" Lamar called out to her.

"I gotta go," she said over her shoulder. "I'll call you later."

Chapter 13

With the strength remaining in her body, Sheena held onto Jah's hand. It was the only thing that kept him calm. Before then, he was snapping off on the hospice home healthcare staff, their aunt, and his friends. Georgia had threatened to have him shot up with a tranquilizer if he didn't act right. He didn't want that. He didn't want to leave his sister's side. So that's where he planted himself.

No one said much to him; they just gave him his space for fear of him going off. He was too emotional for going off at the moment. He did enough of that the first day he walked in and saw his sister at her worst state ever. Now, he just hoped and prayed for a miracle that his sister would somehow get better.

"Do you need something to eat?" Georgia asked.

He shook his head.

"Jah, you gotta eat something," she said.

"I ain't hungry," he mumbled.

"Jah," Nivea said softly as she touched his shoulder tenderly. "You have to maintain your strength."

Jah brushed her hand off his shoulder. "Leave me alone."

Nivea looked over at Georgia. The two women shared a concerned look.

Seconds later, Jazmin and Tanya entered the bedroom.

"Hey ladies," Georgia smiled.

"Hey," Jazmin said. She glanced in Nivea's direction. Jazmin didn't like that she was present but this wasn't the time or the place for any attitudes.

Carefully approaching the side of the bed where Jah was, Jazmin placed a comforting hand on his back. "Are you okay?"

Without looking at her he told her, "Get yo' hand off me."

Jazmin respected his wishes and removed her hand.

Nivea said, "He's not going to talk to you."

"Can I have a moment with him?" Jazmin asked them.

"Sure," Georgia said. "We'll just be right down the hall."

Jazmin waited until they all left before she spoke again. She looked down at Sheena and smiled, "How are you doing?"

Jah answered, "She's fuckin' dying! How the fuck you think she doin'? Damn, get the fuck outta here!"

Sheena squeezed his hand. She actually produce a weak smile for Jazmin. She whispered something that Jazmin couldn't make out.

"Don't talk to her," Jah told his sister. "She dumb as fuck."

Jazmin slapped him on his shoulder. "Stop talking about me like that."

Jah raised up and looked at Jazmin. He asked, "Why the fuck you here?"

"To make sure you were alright," she answered. "I've been trying to get in touch with you but I had no idea this was happening."

"Yeah, cause you too mothafuckin' busy fucking around with Sean's bitch ass," he said.

"I was calling you and texting you, Jah. You never responded."

"Okay Jazmin. You here now. What the fuck you want? I don't need you; didn't ask for yo' ass to be here."

Jazmin reached out to touch him. He slapped her hand away.

"Don't fuckin' touch me. Go touch that nigga atcho house."

"Look, I know you're mad at me but please allow me to be here for you. You're hurting and you're angry at the world. Our differences can be put aside for now. I just wanna be here for you and Sheena," she explained softly.

Jah couldn't help but notice the shimmer of the ring she was wearing. "What the fuck is that?"

Jazmin looked down at her hand and immediately covered the ring. "It's nothing."

"Who gave it to you? Sean?"

"No, but let's not talk about that right now," she said.

"Get out, Jazmin," he said as calmly as he could.

"Jah, Lamar gave it to me but I haven't given him an answer. But what does it matter? You hate me. You don't want me anymore. So why does it anger you?"

"Get yo' dumb ass the fuck outta my sister's room. No, not just her room but get the fuck out of the whole goddamn house, and don't fuckin' come back!"

Jazmin thought about leaving but she couldn't. She took a risk by walking up on him and throwing her arms around him, interlocking her hands together. "I'm not leaving, Jah."

Her closeness, her embrace and persistence broke Jah's defenses. He didn't really want to fight with her. His emotions were just crossed up and he wasn't sure of how he should feel. But he didn't fight her off of him this time. He allowed her to hold him.

"I'm here for you and it's gonna be alright," she said softly.

He tried to speak but she had his face buried in her cleavage.

"What?" she asked.

He pushed her away. "I can't mothafuckin' breathe!"

She started giggling. "I'm sorry."

Sheena coughed and managed a hoarse, "Yay."

Jah cut his eyes at his sister. "That don't mean shit."

Jazmin looked to Sheena and said, "It's a start, right?"

Sheena nodded with her eyes closed.

Jah tore his eyes away from the sight of Jazmin. He was supposed to be grieving his sister's impending death, but he couldn't prevent himself from thinking of how sexy she was in her little black dress. But hell, all of her sexiness was for another man so it didn't even matter.

"Hey! How's my ladybug doing?"

Jah looked up and saw that it was his father. His mood immediately soured again.

Sheena opened her eyes at the sound of her father's voice. She smiled.

"I'ma give yo' ass five minutes," Jah told Dewalis. "When I come back, carry yo' ass on up outta here."

"Jah!" Jazmin scolded.

He ignored her and walked out of the room. He went down the hall to the bathroom. Seconds later when he walked out, he bumped into Jazmin waiting for him. She grabbed him by the arm.

"Are you okay?" she whispered.

"No, I'm not," he answered honestly.

"Maybe I should bring Genesis here," she said.

He managed to finally smile. "That would be nice. I know Sheena would love that."

"I'll have my sister to bring her over."

Jah stared at the ring as Jazmin made the call. Once she ended the call he asked, "What are you gonna tell him?"

"Who?"

"Ol' dude."

"I don't know. He just sprung it on me right before I came here."

"So that's why you all pretty and shit."

"But I ended my date with him just to be here with you."

"And I'm supposed to feel mothafuckin' special?"

"I put you before him, so you should," she said.

"How you gon' take a ring from one nigga but have another nigga atcho mothafuckin' house?"

"Sean?"

"Yeah. Ain't he still there?"

She looked confused. "How did you know he was even there?"

"Oh, it was supposed to be a secret? Ask that nigga. He answered yo' fuckin' phone when I called. I guess he wanted me to know with his bitch ass."

"He what? You called me? When?"

Jah waved her off dismissively. "It don't fuckin' matter. I didn't want shit no mufuckin' way."

"Well, why did you call?"

"It was nothing," he said and walked back into Sheena's bedroom. "Yo' time up mothafucka!"

———

Having Genesis over seemed to give Sheena a small boost of energy. She stayed awake, talked more, and smiled a lot.

When night fell, Jazmin went around saying her goodbyes. She went back into Sheena's now dark room with only a low volume television providing little light. She could see that Jah had fallen asleep in the chair next to Sheena's bed but he was holding a sleeping Genesis in his arms.

"Jazz."

Her voice was soft and raspy barely a whisper. Jazmin walked over to the other side of Sheena's bed. "Yes?"

"Take care of my brother."

"I will."

"Love him."

Jazmin nodded.

"Genesis too."

"Okay."

"He loves you."

"I know," Jazmin said.

"You love him."

Jazmin laughed as tears swelled in her eyes.

"He's sorry."

"I know," she nodded.

"Tell him…"

"What?"

"Tell him…about…baby."

"What baby?" Jazmin asked feeling a little weirded out. How did Sheena know about her pregnancy?

"Baby inside you. He'll…happy."

"I'll tell him."

"Love you."

"Love you—Sheena?"

No response. Panic began to set in. Jazmin whispered again, "Sheena?"

"What?"

Jazmin sighed with relief. "Nothing."

Sheena smiled and drifted off to sleep. Jazmin watched her close for a few seconds to make sure her chest was still rising and falling.

She walked back around to where Jah and Genesis was. She tried to ease Genesis away from him but he held her tighter and instantly woke up in defense mode. "What the fuck you doin'?"

"I'm about to leave," she whispered.

"You coming back?" he asked.

"Do you want me to come back?"

"Hell, I don't want you to leave."

"Will you make up your mind? First you're cussing me out and telling me to leave and now you're asking me not to leave."

"Shutcho ol' juicy ass up," he said playfully.

Jazmin took Genesis from him and placed her carefully in her carrier. "I'll see you tomorrow."

"Jazmin, I don't want you to leave, for real. Stay here with me for tonight," he told her.

She wished she could turn the lights on so she could see how sincere he really was.

He said, "I know you gotta get back to yo' nigga, but just for tonight."

"Why do you think I'm trying to get back to anybody?"

"Cause I'm asking yo' ass to stay but you steady more tryna leave. Tell that gay ass mothafucka you'll see his ass tomorrow."

"Stop calling that man gay," she snickered.

"I guess y'all done fucked now," he said.

"No," she shook her head.

"That nigga still ain't fucked but he giving you rings and shit. What type of shit is that?"

"Jah, he has a few medical problems going on right now."

"Bullshit."

"I'm serious. And one of them is he's having trouble getting and maintaining an erection."

"What?" Jah asked then burst into laughter.

"Ssh!"

"You shouldn't 'ave told me that shit, Juicy! That mothafucka's dick can't get hard! No mothafuckin' wonder yo' ass was throwing that pussy to me."

"Shut up," she whispered. "I shouldn't have told you, you're right. Now don't go saying anything in front of him either."

"Fuck that shit," Jah said. He looked at her with a straight face and bussed out laughing again. "Nigga got a noodle dick! Ol' wobbly sausage mothafucka! Goddamn, he coulda at least ate'cho pussy or something. Damn!"

"Lamar don't do oral sex," she said.

"He what!"

"Shut up, Jah."

"You the one keep telling me this fucked up shit. He don't do oral sex but I bet he suckin' dicks though."

"Jah!"

Teasing her, he said, "I bet yo' pussy hot ain't it? You want some of this dick?"

"Fuck you, Jah."

"That's what I'm tryna offer you," he joked.

She smiled, "I'm glad you're in a better mood and you're able to laugh."

"Thanks for getting Genesis over here," he told her sincerely.

Jazmin sat down on the floor and looked up at Jah. "I think we need to talk about that."

"Why the fuck you on the floor?"

"I didn't wanna disturb Sheena by sitting on her bed," she explained. "But about Genesis…We had sex *that* night, didn't we?"

"We ain't gotta talk about that. We can just leave that shit where the fuck it is. I'm ready to move on from that."

"I agree, but shouldn't we get tested just to make sure?"

"Tested for what? Everybody knows including you; that Genesis is mine. I'm on her birth certificate, I've been claiming her since mothafuckin' day one. That's my baby."

"Okay. But back to *that* night…,"

"What about it, Jazmin? We ain't gotta rehash that shit. We fucked and that's all it was."

"So you remember it vividly?"

"I wasn't drunk; you were."

"And I knew what I was doing?"

"I guess."

"I didn't think I was with Sean did I?"

"Jazmin, you finna make me cuss you the fuck out. Let's leave this shit alone."

"Okay," she said and averted her eyes to the floor.

Jah leaned forward and lifted her face by her chin to face him. "I love you though."

Jazmin smiled and whispered, "I know."

He leaned in further so that he could kiss her lips. He back away to say, "I guess I always will even though you'll never love my ass back. But I'ma let you be happy with the man you want and need in your life. It ain't gon' stop me from being what I need to be for Genni though."

"I know, Jah," she said. She contemplated telling him about the baby. He was at a good place and she'd hate to ruin it but Sheena asked her to tell him about the baby.

"So if you need to get back to yo' man, I'll understand—"

"I'm pregnant," she blurted out.

Jah sat back in his chair. With indifference he said, "Congratulations. Sean know? I know it ain't ol' wobbly sausage ass nigga's baby."

"Jah—" she was saying but was interrupted when Nivea walked in the room.

"Hey bae," Nivea said. "I'm about to go on over to the house. You wanna walk me over?"

Can't this bitch see we're talking? Jazmin thought.

"Yeah, I'll walk you over," Jah said getting up from his chair. He looked down at Jazmin, "I guess I'll see you tomorrow."

Jazmin was left in a state of befuddlement. *What just happened?*

———

The following morning Jazmin was supposed to start her first day of work after maternity leave; however, she called out. She had to make herself available for Jah even though he disregarded her presence.

It angered her that she never got to finish her conversation with him. It bothered her even more to discover that Nivea lived just next door to Georgia. After learning that she assumed that Jah had probably been involved with Nivea the entire time. And then there was still the lady at the condo. *Where did she fit in in all of this?*

Jazmin looked down at the ring Lamar had given her. *Shit,* she thought. He had tried calling her several times the day before while she was at Georgia's. She never accepted any of his calls. But she owed him some type of explanation.

She placed the call and he answered on the second ring.

"Hey baby! I was starting to get worried. Is everything alright?"

"Yeah, I'm okay. But Jah's sister took a turn for the worse and I had to go check on him."

"Oh...Jah," he said with detest.

"Yes, Jah," she said.

"I'm beginning to hate the sound of his name. It seems like whenever I try to move forward with you all I hear is Jah."

"Well Lamar, he's going to be in my life. There's no way around that," she said.

"So what have you decided about the ring?"

She looked at the ring on her finger and removed it. "I think I'm gonna have to give it back to you."

"Why?"

"I just can't right now. And I don't want to accept it and lead you to believe that marriage with you is what I want."

"Oh let me guess...Jah?"

"No...yes...Lamar, I'm pregnant with Jah's baby," she told him.

"No wonder," he said with aggravation.

"No wonder what?"

"Let me ask you this, Jazz; if you weren't pregnant right now would it make a difference?"

"Maybe, but what are you getting at?"

"Do you want to keep it?"

"If you're suggesting an abortion then that's out. Me and Jah may not ever be together as a couple but I won't abort this baby."

"But I can't marry you with another man's baby inside of you."

"I know. And that's why I'm gonna have to say no at this time."

Lamar made a noise to express his devastation. He then said, "Well, can I come by later to get the ring?"

"Sure," she said. "I'll be here."

"How about I bring over some lunch and we can finish talking this out."

"That'll be fine," she said. She heard the sound of her alarm beeping indicating a door had been opened. She hopped out of bed and said to Lamar, "Hey, I gotta go...Call me when you're on the way."

She ended the call absently and placed her phone on her dresser as she headed out of the bedroom. She stood at the top of her stairs and listened. She heard the sound of keys and footsteps getting closer. And just as she was hoping, Jah appeared at the bottom of the stairs.

"What are you doing here?" she asked.

He made his way up the stairs. She could see that he was troubled and his eyes were red and swollen as if he had been crying.

With concern she asked, "Are you okay? Is it Sheena?"

"She ain't opening her eyes," he said. "They said she's slipped into a mothafuckin' coma or some shit. She ain't responding to nothing."

"This happened overnight?" Jazmin asked in shock.

He nodded. "She never woke up."

Jazmin felt so bad for him. She had never seen Jah so down or showing any other emotion besides anger. Seeing him vulnerable softened him and made him normal; not knowing what else to do she embraced him and held him close.

"I'm so sorry, Jah," she said soothingly.

He pushed her away and walked into her bedroom. She stood at the doorway and watched him as he laid across her bed. He was staring up at the ceiling and she could hear him sniffling.

She walked over to her bed and sat down beside him. He was a silent crier as she observed tears flowing from his eyes but trailing down and disappearing into his hairline.

Jazmin lay on her side beside him. He cut his eyes at her and then down at her hand. He asked, "Where's that ring?"

"I took it off. I'm giving it back to him."

"Why?"

"I can't be with him and I'm about to have your baby, Jah."

He didn't say anything. He reached over and touched her belly. "I put another one up in there?"

She smiled. "Yeah, you did."

The same hand that touched her belly he used to caress her face in a tender manner. "My sister was always sayin' life too short for bullshittin' around. She want me and you to be together and she'd be happy than a mothafucka to know we having another baby."

"She knew already. I don't know how, but she did," Jazmin said.

He fondled the diamond heart pendant around her neck. "You sleep in this?"

"I know I shouldn't but I forget to take it off," she said.

Jah pulled Jazmin on top of him. She adjusted herself and hovered over him.

"Do you love me, Juicy?"

She nodded.

"I need you to make me feel good like they say in the movies," Jah said.

She would have laughed but she could see that he was being serious. She lowered her head and covered his mouth with hers. They shared a passionate kiss that made her center ache. She pulled up and looked down at him. "Was that enough?"

"No, I need you to fuck me," he told her.

This was different for Jazmin because when it came to sex Jah was always the aggressor. She let him have his way with her every single time. But the passion she felt for him in the moment drove her to handling her business. And she handled him as tender as she could. After undressing, she undressed him and he lay there, allowing her to make him feel good.

He loosened her hair from its ponytail so that he could grasp her hair in between his fingers as she made love to him with her mouth. When he felt he was on the verge of cumming he yanked her head back.

Jazmin frowned. He chuckled, "My bad...I wasn't ready to cum yet. Climb on top of this dick and fuck me though."

Still frowning, Jazmin positioned herself over him as he helped guide his dick into her wet opening. The way he filled her up was enough to send her over the edge. "Damn Jah."

She lowered her upper body against his and began thrusting onto him.

"This pussy is what I needed," he whispered to her as he grabbed her ass. He assisted her by pulling her to meet his own thrusts.

Jazmin raised her body as his hands slithered up to grope her breasts.

He said, "You feel so good to me, Juicy."

She answered him with moans as she rocked her body. She then adjusted herself so that she was squatting over him with her hands resting on his chest. She started bouncing, allowing his dick to stroke her smoothly.

"Oh shit!" Jah groaned. "That's it baby…Fuck me."

Her legs were on fire but she wanted to push through. Seeing that she was slowing down, Jah decided to take the lead. He raised up and ordered her to lay on her back.

Instead of entering her again he started fucking her with his mouth.

"Oh baby!" she cried out quietly. She grabbed his head and entangled her fingers in his dreads. He was showing her clit no mercy whatsoever. "Fuck!" she hollered.

She started thrusting her hips forward and bringing his head further into her. "I'm about to cum…Oh Jah, baby! I'm cumming!"

A few hard thrusts and she was ready to clamp her legs closed. He moved out of the way before he got trapped. He didn't give her any time to recuperate. He pushed her legs up and started digging in her with an unrelenting passion. She wanted to scream as she fought to let her legs down but he wouldn't let her.

Jazmin couldn't take much more. She understood he was unleashing his frustrations but she could only endure so much. She shoved at his hips and pushed back at the same time. "Fuck, Jah!"

"You want me to stop?"

"No, but—"

"You a big girl. You can take this dick, Juicy," he told her. He pushed her over on her side and positioned himself in between her legs with one thrown over his shoulder. He started pumping in and out of her slowly. Her moans came out as soft whimpers. He bent down to kiss her. "You like that shit, huh?"

"I still hate you," she groaned.

"Don't make me act up in this pussy."

She flashed him a sneaky smile as she closed her eyes. That's all he needed to see before he commenced to putting a pounding on her pussy.

Chapter 14

There were questions Jazmin wanted Jah to answer but she decided to leave it alone for the moment. She wouldn't add any more stress to this already trying time for him.

After showering, she watched Jah put his clothes back on. He went to check on Genesis. Jazmin stood outside Genesis' room and waited for him.

"She still ain't woke up," Jah said. "Whatchu do to her, Juicy?"

Jazmin chuckled, "I didn't do anything. She woke up about five-thirty and wanted to talk."

He joined her in the hallway. "I'm finna head back over to my auntie's house."

"Do you want us to come over?"

"You can but I'll probably be back later," he told her before pecking a kiss to her lips.

"Okay," she said with a smile.

"I love you," he said before heading down the stairs.

"I love you too," she said after him.

Seconds later she was alone again. She went back into her bedroom and picked up her phone to check the time. She had to prepare for Lamar's arrival. After what she shared with Jah, she felt good and confidant about letting Lamar go and giving him his ring back.

After getting dressed for the day and tending to a demanding Genesis, Jazmin received a call from Lamar letting her know he was on his way. As she waited she happened to notice on her call log that the call she had been on earlier with Lamar lasted for about an hour in total. She didn't speak with him that long so that was baffling. Maybe she never hung up but thought she did. *And did he remain on the phone the entire time?*

Lamar arrived shortly after twelve. Despite the ending of their relationship, she still found him to be rather handsome.

"You look nice," she said. "How's work?"

"It's as good as expected," he answered stepping inside her house. He was carrying a cup holder tray with their drinks and an Olive Garden bag.

"You didn't have to bring me lunch," she said.

"Oh, it's no big deal," he said as he made his way towards the den. He took a seat on the sofa and placed the food and drinks on the coffee table.

"I'm not a big fan of Olive Garden," Jazmin said turning up her nose.

He paused from setting the things out and looked up at her, "It's just a salad, Jazz."

She took a seat on the sofa beside him and watched quietly as he set her things in front of her and his in front of him. She grabbed her straw and stuck it in her drink. She took a sip and grimaced, "What is this?"

"You don't like it?"

"It tastes like cherry medicine," she said. She sat it aside and went for her salad.

"It's got acai berry and pomegranate in it. Both are very beneficial health wise. It's not that bad," he said and took of sip of his. "It's actually good for the baby."

"So you say," she said. She reached over and plucked the ring up from the end table and extended it out to him. "Here you go. It's a pretty ring and I'm sure the right woman will love it."

Lamar took it from her and slid in his pocket. "Yeah, I hope so, however, I'm thinking that right woman is still you."

Jazmin shrugged, "Maybe, maybe not."

"I don't plan to give up on us that easily. I mean, I understand you're dealing with some choices to make. I'm willing to back off and let you think things over."

"Yeah," she said and reached for her cup again. She thought about Jah. She asked Lamar, "Did you hang up earlier on our call?"

He looked genuinely confused, "Yeah, why do you ask that?"

She shook her head. "Just wondering." She shuddered at the taste of her drink. She got up and headed for the kitchen.

"What are you doing?"

"Getting some water," she said.

Lamar chuckled, "Jazz, drink the juice. I specifically got this for you. You know what's healthy for us isn't always the tastiest."

"I know but I need some water to chase that down. I guess it takes an acquired taste for it," she said fixing herself a glass of water.

As she sat back down, Lamar asked, "Have you talked to Jah today?"

She looked at him with amusement, "Oh, I thought you couldn't stand the sound of his name yet you speak it from your mouth."

Lamar chewed through his food before speaking. "I know you mentioned something about his sister. I was just wondering if you had heard anything."

"Yeah, I did," she said. "She's gotten worse."

"That's sad to hear," he said.

"And Jah is really messed up behind it."

"So did you tell him about the baby?"

"I did."

"How does he feel about it?"

"He didn't really go all into it but I could tell he was happy about it."

Lamar looked at Jazmin's food and drink. "Hmmm…maybe that's a good thing. Eat and drink up."

———

On his way back to his aunt's house Jah decided to make a stop to check on Erica. He hadn't really heard from her since he was at her house last.

He told her to keep him updated about her pregnancy but she hadn't bothered to call him and tell him anything.

When he drove up a frown instantly covered his face. He thought he was surprising her by dropping in but he was the one getting surprised. Without question, he immediately knew who's red Challenger was sitting in her driveway. *Why in the fuck was Sean at Erica's?*

Against his better judgment to just go to his aunt's house, Jah parked along the neighbor's front yard and made his way to Erica's front door. He remembered she had given him his key back a while ago even though he hadn't used it. He took it out and slipped it in her lock. *Dumb bitch, didn't even get the locks changed*, he thought as he let himself in.

Stepping into the living room, he observed that she hadn't cleaned in days. There were so many piles of clothes that he almost didn't notice her kids in the living room with their eyes glued to the television. They had big bowls of cereal in front of them with the milk and various boxes of cereal on the floor beside them.

"Where y'all mama at?" Jah asked. They all turned to him as if seeing a strange man was nothing new to them.

The elder of the three pointed upstairs. "She up there."

Jah crept upstairs quietly and could hear them talking before he got close to her bedroom door.

"Sean! Get up!" Erica was saying.

"Woman, I'm hurting right now. Leave me the fuck alone…damn," Sean murmured.

"You need to take ya' ass back to Rayven," Erica said.

"So your ass can harass me and beg me to come back? Shut up, Erica."

"You shut up. You need to be spending some quality daddy son time with DeSean. He don't' even know who you are."

"I am, later on. You need to clean this house! Got my son up in here like this."

"Well why don't you take him and let him live with you and Rayven in your fancy house in the suburbs, nigga!"

"I told you I'm here with you now."

"Whatever. You want me to bring you something back up here?" she asked.

"Something to drink," he told her.

Erica yanked her bedroom door open and almost shitted herself when she saw Jah standing right there.

"Go back in the room," Jah told her in an even tone.

Erica backed up with her mouth dropped open in fear.

Sean looked up, "Who's that?"

"Look, Jah, I can explain!" Erica was saying but Jah grabbed her by her neck and pushed her out of the way.

Sean sat up instantly. "Jah, look man, it ain't—"

All Jah could see was red; all he wanted to see was red. Red from anger and red leaking from Sean. He didn't even give Sean the opportunity to stand up before he started pummeling him. Erica was hysterical and trying to get Jah to stop. She grabbed Sean's gun that was tucked under the pillow and aimed it at Jah.

"If you don't stop and get the fuck outta my house I will shoot yo' ass!" Erica threatened. "I'll teach you 'bout putting your hands on me!"

"Bitch, I ain't put my hands on you, yet!"

"I'll blow your mothafucking head off if you do!"

Jah trampled over Sean's unconscious body and went after Erica. "You gon' do what? Bitch, shoot me!"

Trembling, Erica backed away but stumbled on some clothes on the floor. He got out of the bed and stood over her yanking the gun from her at the same time. "I oughta bash yo' mothafuckin' head in with this shit! You fucked with yo' life bitch! You and this nigga is dying today! Go say bye to yo' goddamn ugly ass kids, bitch!"

———

It was later in the day when Jazmin was called over to Georgia's house. Fearing the worst, she prepared herself before she walked in. The atmosphere was solemn. Even the hospice care team was in melancholic states.

Georgia greeted Jazmin with a hug and took Genesis from her. She pointed towards Sheena's room. "He's in there."

Jazmin walked by some of their family members to get to Sheena's bedroom. She was at a loss for words when she saw Jah crying his heart out in his sister's bed with what was only a shell left of Sheena's existence. Jazmin didn't know what to do. She walked over to him and started rubbing his back. When he realized it was her he turned to her and wrapped his arms around her and cried.

"She's gone," he wept.

"I know," Jazmin cried with him as she continued to rub him soothingly.

Georgia stood in the doorway and mouthed to Jazmin, "Get him out of the bed."

Jazmin nodded. She looked at the people from the coroner's office waiting in the room "C'mon Jah, we gotta let the people do their jobs."

"No."

"Baby, they gotta take her," she explained. She looked over at how peaceful Sheena looked. She was just as angelic as she was when she was alive. Jazmin could tell that she was happy when she took her last breath.

Suddenly, Jazmin felt nauseous and a severe pain surged through her stomach. She ignored it because she had to focus on Jah.

Then there was a bunch of commotion coming from down the hall.

"Now wait a minute!" Leon could be heard yelling.

"Sir," an authoritative voice boomed through the air. "You're interfering with law enforcement. I'm gonna have to ask you to step aside."

Georgia looked down the hallway at three police officers approaching. "What's the problem?"

"We're looking for a Jabari Bradford," the shorter of the three officer said.

Jazmin looked down at Jah with widen eyes. "What did you do?"

Jah ignored the question and told her, "I love you and I'm sorry, okay?"

"Sorry for—" she was interrupted as another pain shot through her stomach. "Something's not right!"

"What the fuck you mean?" Jah asked. There was a mixture of concern, fear, anger, sadness and devastation etched across his face.

"I think I'm—"

"Jabari Bradford!" the booming voice officer said into the bedroom.

"What did he do?" Georgia asked frantically. "Can't you see we're having a family crisis right now! My niece, his sister just died!"

Jah didn't acknowledge the police officers. He was concerned with Jazmin. "Baby, what's wrong?"

The one officer stepped to him, "Jabari Bradford, you're under arrest."

Jah screamed at the officer, "For what?"

Booming voice officer stepped in to try to strong-arm Jah because Jah wasn't going to just cooperate.

"Jah, don't fight!" Rita hollered from the hallway. "Oh Lord! Mama, do something!"

"What's he being arrested for?" Georgia demanded.

After a small little scuffle, booming voice officer managed to slap the cuffs on Jah's wrists. "Do you want another charge for resisting!"

"Nigga, fuck you!" Jah spat.

"You're under arrest for bodily assault, unlawful entry, assault with a firearm, and attempted murder on an Erica Lewis and Sean

Simmons," the other officer said and began reading Jah his rights.

"Jah!" Jazmin cried out. She looked at the officers desperately, "Can you please leave him. His sister is right here, dead!"

"Ma'am, these are serious charges," the short one said. "Once he's been booked and bail set, you and your family can get him out."

"You insensitive mothafuckas!" Georgia hollered out.

Jazmin watched hopelessly as they shoved Jah out of the room. She started vomiting and doubled over in pain. *This couldn't be happening*, she thought. She knew what she was experiencing; she was losing the baby.

To Be Continued

Acknowledgments

First and foremost, I must acknowledge and give a major shout out to all of my readers! You guys rock and made CRUSH one of my most successful pieces of work. Just know that without you guys, I wouldn't be so driven and motivated. I love being stalked for my follow up work. And trust me, you all have done a phenomenal job of stalking! Love it! I appreciate all of the love and support you guys have shown in making CRUSH a #1 Bestseller.

I have to make some specific shout outs to readers Yolanda Morgan, Carmen Doster Johnson and Kimberly Olds Artis. I'm so glad to have become acquainted with these ladies! They're the best! Oh and major shout out to the Facebook Bookclub I LOVE TO READ AND CAN'T HELP IT! Hey complainers! Much love! Wendy Sherod and Denise Henson, I swear you ladies are awesome. Every time I turn around you're tagging me because you're spreading the word on my work! Much appreciated! And Delores Miles...what can I say? You've been there since day 1 encouraging me and praising my work along the way. Love you lady!

To my publisher Tremayne Johnson...Thank you! It's been and is a pleasure being with you. I think you're awesome and you're wonderful at what you do. I'm going to keep saying that. KEEP doing you! Most importantly, you believe in my work and have nothing but encouraging words to say. Thank you. To the rest of my King Publishing Group/Tremayne Johnson Presents family...what's up?

And last but not least, my sister friends Faith, Shalonda, Tameka, Jasmine, and Sunny. Soooo glad to have you guys in my corner. Love yall!

Most importantly, I'd like to thank my mother Brenda Lockett, my cousin Geneva Mitchell, daughter India Bradford and my awesome friend Kent Braden for being encouraging and believing in me. Love you guys! Oh, and hey to my little ones Harrah, AJ, and Dion just because. I know I've tuned yall out while I was writing but uhm...yeah...Get in there and boil them hot dogs up! Lmao! Love you!

41211545R00157

Made in the USA
Middletown, DE
06 March 2017